SUSPECT M
THE CASE OF THE MISSING PATIENT

ALEKSANDRA MCHUGH

Published by
Eleusinian Press Ltd
www.eleusinianpress.co.uk

All rights reserved

No part of this book may be reproduced in any form by photocopying or any electronic or mechanical means, including information storage or retrieval systems, without permissions in writing from both the copyright owner and the publisher of the book.

First Edition published 2018
© Aleksandra McHugh

Printed and bound in Great Britain
by Copytech (UK) Ltd

A catalogue record for this book
is available from The British Library

ISBN 978-1-90949X-XX-X

THE PENETRATED ASYLUM/DR. CREPITUS PRESIDING

"Of human sacrifice, and parents tears,
Though, for the noyse of Drums and Timbrels loud,
Their children's cries unheard that passed through fire
To his grim Idol. Him the AMMONITE
Worshipt in RABBA and her watry Plain,
In ARGOB and in BASAN, to the stream
Of utmost ARNON. Nor content with such
Audacious neighbourhood, the wisest heart
Of SOLOMON he led by fraud to build
His Temple right against the Temple of God
On that opprobrious Hill, and made his Grove
The pleasant Vally of HINNOM, TOPHET thence
And black GEHENNA call'd, the Type of Hell."
– John Milton, *Paradise Lost*

"Porn is hell."
– Susanna Breslin, *Exquisite Corpse*

A dolly swung out over the exercise yard proclaims BULLET POINT PRESENTATION. Episode One. The penetrated asylum.

"The nature of which is speculative at present," recites Dr. Crepitus, the asylum's head psychoanalyst.

"Yes, speculative. We are exactly that pandering. Let us start at the shallow end and ease in.

Consider this the rehearsal dinner where we blow the cobwebs out before wedding our tilting vessel to her mad ship's captain. Together, unto the watery grave. That final test, will she swim or will she drown (Joyce or his daughter? You can only save one!), made famous by our phantom hysteric, now unhappily repressed, that most notorious Black Beast of Medicine.

But first, who is she, our vessel, to be? Is she behind a veil? Does she dare wear white? Perhaps a toast. A christening to launch our last tour of the love cure. She merges with various suitors before she's nailed down in our museum. Perhaps some introductions. Let us dub our first exhibit Lucy A., from our above-ground collection."

[Now reading from the overhead].

"An early history of forcible confinement and cruel experiment, given over to successive reforms, our ward then deinstitutionalized, defunded, left to her own degenerative devices—a brief stay in our all-female deviant wing—now fully integrated in a most opportune coalescence of austerity and fluidity.

Yes, our formerly over-subscribed ward, having been put through the wringer, has now entered the past-prime, criminal portion of the dating cycle. Think weed dealer with a 'Scarface' complex and extensive weapons collection. Think South African cigarette smuggler whose heart is an ice pick. Think a Handler who is connected. This new breed of suitor that skulks beneath the sultry orb of cathexis in mortido. Death wish. Still waiting for Mr. Goodbar; maybe he arrives this time, so the gavel finally drops, but until then, Quel Suspense!

This peculiar vintage does lend her an aura of mysterious terrere. We are beset upon by those who would exploit the residual fascination with her tortured past. (Overdub: You might be done with the wringer, but the wringer isn't done with you.) This interest is piqued by rumours of some unsavory business being conducted in our snaking bowels of tunnel and antechamber, the extant sewers and isolation cells, the operating rooms that are vestige to a perverse science.

'Ooh, what is he doing in there?' they whisper in the grocer. Let them have a look, curious townsfolk with their ever-ready pitch forks. For a price. We endeavour to satisfy their lust for private detail, as we do for the medical establishment that is ever frothing with envy over our special relationship with this the most difficult of patients who they cast off as incurable."

[Sliding the shaft of his riding crop up the frame of the basement opening dramatically].

"It is here, in these confounding tunnels, that one most senses an accumulation of disturbed energy! We are clearly in some border region between this world and the next.

Still, what is really unsettling is that this primary patient thinks herself some sort of lay analyst. [In a high-pitched imitating voice] 'I do emotional innovations,' she announced during intake and clearly intends to sabotage our therapeutic relationship. This lay tendency is the final nail in a psychoanalysis now widely regarded as decadent charlatanism, with my asylum being carved into miserly chunks to be hung out in the market as so much meat for wild dogs. Yet, the university persists in churning out new graduates, bloody martyrs as I like to call them, only too willing to dance for peanuts. All of us are squeezed into what is merely a more respectable tier of precarity and suspended in this layer of resin. Hence, my dual role as a ghostly adventures tour guide. You do what you have to, really. That's my ethic, if I have one.

Of course, there are less vampiric beneficiaries of the asylum's vivisection into useable parts. A damaged quadrant of the Brodmann's areas 25, 10 and 11 is now converted into a film set by some lovely students who mean to incorporate our medieval esthetic into their paranormal documentary. Just due to the revival of those. 'The Mystery of the Missing La Bete Noir' they're calling it, after our own phantom.

I am only too pleased to heighten the forbidding atmosphere. In fact, I think you'll find I have a flare for the theatric myself and have been told I bear uncanny resemblance to the great Charcot. Not to give too much away, but my greatest contribution to the legacy of the love cure is what I call the erotomanic trauma reenactments. Allow me to demonstrate."

[Serious face]. "This cannot be called progress, this vivisection. It is not even the progression of slingshot to atom bomb. All the implements stay the same, repurposed. We are in the standstill, the trade in flesh, that fourth currency into perpetuity. We are always in the right place at the right time for such accoutrements. There is no time here, but only accumulations and recombining features. It's a simulation, in other words.

Still, if you were to step right up to almost puncturing this fourth abutment, this film, you will see it is not just some no-strings, make-believe fun zone. Never mind the nostalgic disco balls and tickle trunk. Never mind the party favours. This is a realist exhibition. A genealogy of tops and bottoms in micro-minis.

SUSPECT M

Neither has our repressive armor simply dissolved in a tub of acid. We are as rigid as ever. The only access to deeper levels is through heavy cellar doors, these further impeded by re-naturalized gardens that slope downward in a continuous relay into forest. Or, it's a national park of contested jurisdiction and a disproportionate number of disappearances Just compared to other forests, other national parks. If you were to murder someone here, for instance, you wouldn't be accountable to any authority. I mean technically, legally. Indeed, a certain conspiratorial patient of mine, Sid M., claims us to be a sort of triangular vortex for missing persons who are to be made slaves in the next world. Ha! An exaggeration I assure you. A little notoriety never hurt anyone's bottom line.

But yes, he is that paranoid. The world is his microorganism and he takes it VERY personally, as do most of the wards in our exhibit. But just because they are doesn't . . . That saw. That electric fuzzy for your fears. Another treatment we may or may not provide here, with metal clamps and cables. It's a MYSTERY. You will have to come on one of paid tours to find out.

One thing is certain. This facility is haunted. This can be sussed by the usual sounds and sightings, the rasping and rales, the creaking and popping, by what can be sensed just out of reach, especially in those frictive areas where we are not at all certain if it is merely a matter of worn down cartilage or actual fracture, or whether these may be crystalline in nature so as to break along certain, predetermined fault lines.

Right, frictive.

It's the adjacent graveyard, generations of patients and staff alike, having lived and died on these grounds. Or, it's the stone wall forest abutment, the missing patients. Some of them escapees, due to the usual institutional attrition, others aged out or moved along, gone on nature hikes never to return. Or, it's possible we've simply misplaced their files. Try running a last-ditch asylum before you judge. We can't be expected to keep track of everyone. I mean, do you want us monitoring your every move, or don't you? Make up your minds sheeple! Sorry, that's a joke at the expense of Sid. We are not without humour at our asylum.

Don't moral panic or anything, but what we know of these original, eternal inhabitants is that they were often poor, victimized by not only whatever mental infirmities they possessed, but on various scores by a society that was repelled by them or merely wished not to see them except behind glass and on vacations of the senses.

One thing is certain. This will get much much worse before it gets better. Just due to the subgrade loops and no light at both ends, so you just have to keep going. Your only fidelity is to that distant drumbeat; you will follow it follow it wherever it may go.

That's the nature of this curing impulse. It's a hard-core spiritual journey and bearing witness. That part's true. I've seen footage.

And, if in the final wash she is psychotic and sinks, our ward, having failed to renew her subscription to the unconscious, well then, that will be a resolution too. There will be no meanings to fetch up. They will all be right there on the surface for everyone to see, naked in front of the computer."

***

LUCY A. CROSSES THE THRESHOLD/ THE FACILITY IS INTEGRATING

"There is a strange, uncomfortable, somewhat inhuman feeling to her. It feels somewhat like having a dream with an archaic figure who speaks in a stilted language from a distinct century yet carries a strong affect. She speaks to me in plain English, has affects I clearly recognize, is suffering, and yet also seems inhuman, of a different species. Her words carry a fullness that feels like they each link to a greater whole, yet they are expressed in a strangely shallow manner. Alternatively, she has great depth and insight. Still, each moment is strained, too full and also too empty. She seems an outcast, living on the fringes of the world, cast into a dark shadow of inhuman archetypal processes and speaking through them as if she were partaking of a human dialogue. She seems a princess, a witch, a clown, a trickster. We are in a fairy world of abstract characters which quickly turn back to blood and flesh reality. I am left feeling guilty for ever thinking her anything other than genuine."
– Janet Wirth-Cauchon, Sociologist (citing an un-named psychiatrist) *Women and Borderline Personality Disorder*

ALEKSANDRA McHUGH

[Lucy speaks]

"It's been a while since I first embarked on my perilous journey of online dating to cure my love addiction. At first it seemed an allurement to the intensification of life. My 'Love Addict' handle chosen over the more accurate, but cumbersome, 'disorganized attachment and pseudo-hypersexuality as features of borderline personality' to appeal to an audience suckled on a steady drip of internet Pablum. Not to be insulting, but there will be no more such pandering, that quest now suspended in favour of something more well-cloistered and I have to switch tacks.

Consider the above assessment from my doctor–that it might serve to force intimacy–and you will instantly care what happens to me. It's just that I do now find myself in desperate need of an ally or at least someone who means me no harm. So, if that sounds like you, let's chat! During proper visiting hours. Hint, hint. That's a clue as to my current predicament.

I'm still on the dating app, which I've renamed 'Abundant Dick' just because . . . no reason, and despite its religious use, my perfect match eludes me. Not just by ignoring messages and hiding behind bushes. They're wrong about these attachments. They can't latch just anywhere and had, at one point, sought out those avoidant of love. It just has a certain symmetry. A mirror quality. It presents a certain masochistic opportunity to hook into the weakest parts of another's psyche and repeat early trauma. Or, in this case, a deep and broad-seated neglect, longstanding rejection, and assault, culminating in a very dramatic scene where you're collapsed in a puddle spasm on their lap begging, 'Please don't leave me in the reeds again mommy.' after which your spirit is rent, pining for your other half, who's really just not that into you.

It was with full knowledge (he showed me what he was, and I believed him) that I sat at my chosen avoidant's feet, eyes lowered, waiting for him to fetch something from my mouth (some bird), or command me to perform some task (turn the pages of his book). That was a very long day of distance and waiting, eons. I said, 'I like it this way., the nature of my subjection and precarity, disregard the knuckles.'

I was a good secretary and he was a good pariah doggie. As good as one can be. But, on the next day he was sniffing up other trousers, trying to entice a teenager. I contorted myself into unnatural shapes (a set of slavering red lips, not my style at all) to please him. To fail to please him.

For this, I was shut outside the land of faeries in my place in dissociated arrangements. That night, I reassembled myself into a set of murderous claws and slashed him to bits. Then I begged forgiveness and the world was renewed again, the two of us a furious band of reactivity in a ring around its core.

That's what happens when no one is true bottom but only adopting it as a therapy module. When you are only pretending, as in a ploy to trick a wolf into playing your grandmother. Your only recourse then, as it has always been, the magical thinking of mistreated children. If I am to be punished, it will be by my own hand. It will be because I am nearly unbearable. You think you can drive me crazy? Well, I can drive you more. Right up to the lip and almost kissing.

As you might expect that dating cycle did not resolve well. Even aside from my preoccupation with a lover who was always surreptitiously inching toward the door. Well, not total preoccupation. I was at the same time apportioning my affection amongst several other deserving suitors. Moreover, it landed me in an abandoned asylum fresh out of break or retreat with intractable case of globus hystericus. Tongue-tied and a red ball lodged my throat. Blocked. Which my so-called analyst deemed willful faking.

That predictable ending. That ending predicted. You're on your own. And then hitting yourself several times in the head with it echoing, 'You're on your own You're on your own You're on your own You're on your own.' Like a saint who is a self-judge with a gavel in a tunnel chamber. My former pariah doggie now turned a penal guard at the very borderline facility I'm now in which I am housed in! His once excitedly flapping tail become a flaccid baton of 'doesn't know me' and 'professional distancing'.

Yes, those spells were aimed at me. I know because I fell into a pit of undulating snakes like roots that threaded down my throat, a mercury-filled balloon, a plug, a clot. And all while AWAKE. Which, you're right, is a lot like drowning. While prying my death grips from his encrusted armour, he said 'If you think I have the power to redeem you, that's a problem.' Ipso facto chango. That's the problem of my damnation. UNREDEEMABLE.

The cop that turned the wrong way. Counter-revolution. And who apparently was right that these are not the times for a Russell Brand messiah complex. Never mind the yoga pants and hipster-settler moustache. He's NOT GOING TO HELP YOU, he's meditating. Yay self-therapies!

So ensued a period of isolation and ignoring. Yes, it turns out you CAN ignore us, Dan. A period of ruminating and finally elucidating that however perfectly suited we might be for a murder-suicide, I don't really like avoidants. Or, let's just call them what they are, emotional anorexics. Everybody on a starvation diet. That's not very innovative. Okay maybe it is. Still, you don't really want to be nested in someone's gullet in a state of parasitic symbiosis. Like starving. Or drowning. Or.

Out of this was instituted a new policy. Avoid the avoidant. Consider it cautionary. I do. Any nascent encounters since, I have snuffed in the cradle. If that's not an alarming image! Still necessary, I assure you. Let them cast about elsewhere for their food supply that is never satisfying, fussy toddlers.

Except 'avoidant' is wrong. They are, rather, on the intermittent schedule of the narcissist. Flashing over-responsive at first, they love bomb you. But then, at unpredictable intervals, flashing hostile, indifferent, flashing feather bed dropped out and in its place a sheet of ice. That's the real cycle. Underneath any apparent cleverness and fixing problems, the real compulsive law is being laid down in planks of coldness and cruelty that will, one day, dispassionately tip you into the sea and watch you flail until, lungs flooded, you sink."

* * *

HIS DEATH DRIVE/THE POST-ZED TURN

"There is a malignant type of self-destructiveness, which we will see in a small group of our patients, and which is, I think, in the nature of an addiction – an addiction to near-death. In their external lives, these patients get more and more absorbed into hopelessness and involved in activities that seem destined to destroy them physically as well as mentally. It is not as a drive towards a Nirvana type of peace or relief from problems. Indeed, just to die, although attractive, would be no good. There is a felt need to know, and to have the satisfaction of seeing oneself being destroyed."
– Betty Joseph, *Addiction to Near-Death*

"Cut to the chase scene, a teaser. You are inside the wolf this time, pre-eaten, pre-abandoned, yet still dogged across the tracks and into the forest because this is your Ultimate Date! This is a matter of letting the right one in. Isn't it always? It is what I should have done in the first place and saved everyone a lot of DRAMA. Sorry everyone! The right one being the one who won't LET you leave. It's a very secure facility. It's driving in the wrong direction of your home with the doors locked asking, 'Are you scared?'

SUSPECT M

Let us hope that this remedy within a therapeutic context will bring satisfaction so as to avoid the further staging of some Theresa Dunn or Edith Cadiz burial scenario.

Just because you have a death wish doesn't mean you want to die. That would be a crude misinterpretation of the teachings of the doctor and his cohort. Should anyone fall prey to treachery, in this universe or any other, it is a set-up, a sink trap, prey. A matter of preying really hard for something, of wishing and hoping and planning and, well, maybe it arrives this time, this stuffed wolf. You get the picture; it's very circular. That's the nature of fixation. You are on pause and held in a formula.

How cavalier I was in the beginning about all my bad dates. I mean, what a lark! Behold my youthful verve! Until it was impressed upon me the true meaning, the obvious meaning, of bad dates, that was possibly apparent to everyone but me.

Yes, so now I have other problems, worse problems. And surrounding these, an aura of malign intent. It's hard to separate real from unreal threats when you have a water-witch perceptiveness that verges on paranoia.

Not to say I'm confused about anything that really happens. I'm still not in Russia and we can go for coffee. Not like that. But only in terms of intentions. And how certain worse realities might pertain to me. And what magical qualities I might possess to bring these about. Just as I had previously claimed to resist abandonment while frantically priming the spring of my own catapult, I now suspect myself of pursuing my own demise.

Or, maybe, that's a device of some sort, to first get persons to pay attention to some more troubling content by lure of a nymphet who is blithely fornicating her way along a crest of weird, but uniformly cis men unaware of the machinations she is caught up in until suddenly, smack in the face of the second , abuse half, of a documentary as a COMPLETELY DIFFERENT ACTRESS. How is that not shocking, Lars Von Trier? And now, in her mid-forties (and no matter which internet misogynist you ask, she is WAY past prime) her un-pristine body (or it could be her face) somehow justifies the launch of the criminal portion of her dating cycle.

Whatever the impetus, it's undeniable, this new tedious morass I'm in, with ropey lengths that are not dissolved by simple wish or spell but want something more elaborate. A stratagem.

That's the crux of the problem, if there is one. Here, I mean. The whole point of therapy, as I see it, is to transfer that problem, whatever twist of a dense knot you are in, worriedly going over and over again, to some secondary platform, be it art or religion, so as to transfigure it. No, probably not into gold–this being the religious platform, obviously. But something. Because I believe in it.

In as much as I once so believed in my aversive power, that the universe has determined to correct it, and is now overcorrecting in my opinion.

I had long felt that way, possessed of an aversiveness, like a Carrie or a Firestarter. Two-faced and of cursed fate. Forged by a crucible of bullies and untouchable. "Those who feel me near pull the blinds and change their minds." That line from a cat musical.

It seemed a joke, an impossible joke, when first I said that as a love addict, having just been ceremoniously dumped with much poetry, that what I might really, really want is someone who refuses to leave. Consider my surprise when I should find myself not only abandoned but confined, and in successive near-confinements.

SUSPECT M

So now for the seamless sashay to the second location of my cautionary tale in which I recur. Motifs always recur. That's the nature of fixation. We repeat what we don't understand in cycles. But also, what we know very well. It's very episodic. It's very stutter shock. And all around you, voices. This facility is integrating, which can be very disorienting and dysmorphic, in which case, you will want to discern a logos and get your bearings."

AN IRREAL MAP OF THE FACILITY/LUCY UPON ENTERING LUCIDLY

"The first thing to depart in a mental breakdown is the familiar."
– Philip K. Dick, *Valis*

"On first impression, this abandoned asylum is buttressed on all sides by uncanny near-encounters with horror. It's a particular brand I am not a fan of at all. My dating cycle has definitely hit a rough patch, its criminal portion felt as a sharp zigzag in the road. I am now in the bend of certain motifs and there is no going back. It's just not my way to do that. I have always been very tenacious in that respect, following whatever rivet I am in through to its catastrophic ending. Consider that an attribute.

At first, I saw three figurations. Without warning. Or, they were their own warning. It was through some sort of observation window; now I am responsible for them. That's a superstition. Lest they should haunt me. Or go unwitnessed.

The presiding physician says, 'Don't worry, this is all a simulation.' But, what could that mean? That it's all pretending? That this is the secondary platform and we are all pretending here? All I can say is congratulations to whoever the God of this place is, then. Because the scenes were VERY convincing.

SUSPECT M

And their participants were VERY good actors, despite any low-budget and underground production values.

They also seemed to condense whole worlds, as signs encoded in the rubbery twists of an ancient root bound up in luminous coils, wanting to be pried apart and understood. So then let the horrors unfold gradually, like snakes.

I can't speak of them directly. But I can sense their inhabitants just beyond a partition. In places, it's a thin separation, as a film or membrane, a threat you are pressed up against that could burst. Not that you would mean to, but… Your body then thrown onto an accumulating pyre of what? Mutilated paper cut-out dolls.

From any point in this borderline facility, you can feel the heat of this furnace that extends into underground tracts that are said to be its financial engine. There are many dispersed supply centres actually, a ductwork of subsidiary channels.

Feeding into it are wider strips, runs of Broadway nights spent in futile attempts to allay loneliness, as you do out in the yard by daylight. Such fraternizing is ostensibly free ranging, though you are cordoned in, a red-lined holding pen. The neglected garden is more sprawling and slopes downward as an unbroken relay into forest, a thickly obscured shadowy region where bad things cycle inevitably as in a true fairytale. That seems to be the point of it, that the transition is so gradual you will hardly notice when you are suddenly on a treacherous plane.

In fact, there is a patient here, a Sid M., who speaks of breakaway tunnels inhabited by all the missing persons who are to be slaves in the next world. I can't help but wonder if what he perceives isn't breakaway at all, but existing among us in a subliminal realm where, when consent forms had been signed at all, it was under duress. Or no one wants to buy you except for. Or do you want to be a model?

The neglected garden is like its own society, open-air. The forest is at the opposite end of your confinement where you are safe, though being drained of content. And why wouldn't you prefer that? Why would you flirt with horror instead, or worse pursue it, so that it is almost becoming a lifestyle with you? Why wouldn't you just turn back around and go the other way, if you could?"

***

A DOCTOR'S NOTE ON SID M./HIS BAND OF MISCREANTS

"They're building a case concerning my perversity," said Sid M. in our first session, launching into his extended grievance. First referred by his employer following an incident of alleged touching, this unfortunate believes himself a patsy in a breakaway society scheme involving missing persons of the underground tunnel variety. It is a transfer of his sexual difficulties and precarious job situation to the realm of fantasy, no doubt, with these being expressed through a stream of inexplicable tics and bodily ailments, irrational fears, obsessive and intrusive thoughts, and generally self-punishing behavior. Although he is under investigation for numerous indiscretions; so it's not entirely off the mark.

The first of these is the touching, what Sid claimed was an accident, but which could only be an unconscious wish inopportunely expressed. The infraction then placed on his permanent file with the temp agency, and Sid on probation until he could undergo assessment and sensitivity training. He was already oversensitive.

It was around the same time that he was accused of violating a statute governing rooming houses, some arcane "spouse in the house" rule that remained on the books. Still, rules are rules. He had subsequently been ordered to appear before a tribunal. Informally, there were rumblings about his inadequate performance of communal duties, i.e., lawn care. Further, his coworkers were uncomfortable with his practice of carrying a note pad to the staff room. He appeared to be observing them, they said. Management had talked to him several times about his ill-fit with workplace culture, citing his outmoded burner phone (the kind associated with drug dealers), his preference for riding a bicycle (and lack of a car), his habit of bringing his own box cutter to work, and the fact that his close friend and co-worker had gone missing.

Added to this, the patient is possessed of a partially sublimated "Scarface" complex and is stockpiling weapons. These, he says, are defensive in nature. Still, it's best he not feel threatened, for example by challenging the veracity of his beliefs, which merely serves as evidence that you, too, were "in on it,", if that's not disconcerting.

Indeed, amongst his weapons, as if to carry the weight of an enormous sin, melee of flagellation gear loaded up his wiry frame. His body turned into a polluted temple of depravity. Inordinately guilty. Unless rumours linking him to the missing young woman had substance.

Even so, it is his florid ideation that is most striking, even if typical. Caught up in that hornet's spire of cynical suggestibility that had infected so large a contingent of young men that in another century it would have been deemed a religious epidemic, the sufferers then rounded up like punch-drunk cattle. Luckily, these are more humane times where we take care of our psychically addled. Lucky for Sid, my asylum doors are always open, the generous bosom of a neighborly washer woman who takes in everyone else's rejects despite the financial burden on her own household.

Amongst his fantasies is what he calls the establishment's dissociative identity experiments–or DIDs–which are apparently part of a vaster conspiracy to manufacture mind-controlled slaves.

As is characteristic of its imagined victims, he switches between nearly distinct personalities, the primary one being reminiscent of someone undergoing a trial. This serves to heighten his sense of being pursued by some malignant entity outside himself. He attributes his every vile impulse to this foreign assault with little insight into his own rejected desires and instincts. Meanwhile, he remains blind to the true source of his trauma which seems to lie in extensive bullying during his youth, most severely at the hands of his father.

Whatever the seeds of his defensive overgrowth, he regards his arsenal as a sort of security blanket. The asylum had therefore permitted him to keep it, along with his thick of file of evidence against his employer. It is my opinion that to take these away would unleash an all-out war. We must first get him to step back from the ledge.

At present, he questions the motives of everyone around him. "Why would they assign me to a pharmaceutical company with my history of addiction? It could only be to occupy me and police my activities. Did you know they subjected me to drug tests? Did they imagine me anything but fully compliant during the daylight hours of the workplace? Of course, everywhere else too and even in my dreams."

On and on goes his litany. "Then why the unmistakable scent of guilt, Sid? And would you be a peach and wash the communal shower afterward?" I dared not say these outright, though. Sid waits for someone else to pull the pin on his tightly-wound rage. We don't want to be that someone, do we?

However confused, he is a compelling character. Due to his extreme presentation his atrocity of flesh, he attracts quite a following in the yard. A band of miscreants against the governing order, primed to doubt all authority in favour of peculiar subjectivity. He has gathered around him all manner of battle-scarred trauma cases, casualties of unauthorized drug experiments, of psychic bombardments designed to fracture and boggle. It's the building back up that's harder. Out of their derangement sprung a schema, a movement, a deep storehouse of supporting documents. But to what end? Hitched to what rallying cry? Something about a beta slave uprising if I have correctly gleaned something from their literature.

Partly as a result of Sid's influence, I now have several patients on the brink, differently on the brink, convinced of this institution's fraudulence, and mine. What's more, he has an associate called The Handler, which is never a good sign.

* * *

LA SALPETRIERE REVISITED BY TOURISTS

"Veritable actresses, they do not know a greater pleasure than to deceive . . . all those with whom they come in touch. The hysterics who exaggerate their convulsive movement . . . make an equal travesty and exaggeration of the movements of their souls, their ideas, and their acts . . . in a word, the life of the hysteric is nothing but one perpetual falsehood; they affect the airs of piety and devotion and let themselves be taken for saints while at the same time abandoning themselves to the most shameful actions."
– Jules Falret on the hysterics of Charcot's *La Salpetriere*.

Just days before opening, Crepitus is giving a closed-circuit dry run of the facility's basements to the first test audience, and skeleton crew. With everyone congregated on the stone steps to enter front-wise, it is somewhat congested.

The widening boom careens off a strappado in the atrium-cum-gift shop, sending a shiver through a Candi Staton cover of "Nights on Broadway" that's being pumped in at deafening levels. In florescent bug-eyed yellow, a sign flashes WARNING.

The doctor's voice breaks through the surround. "Standard operating procedure," he says. It's a non-stop disco. "We'll have to suspend the audio during this portion of the tour and pick it up later. Yes, that's a thing, noise asylum, breaking point, look it up.

Some people find this leg unsavory, but it helps with the bills. You do what you have to, really. You're enterprising. I prefer that, if I'm being honest, to think of it as an enterprise as opposed to 'this whole affair or something', which sounds compromising. I don't like the word 'affair'. It reeks of casting couch. We are not that kind of facility. I definitely don't like this jaunty organ grinder cap I'm expected to wear in precise rotation. Admit it, colleagues, organ grinder is an ethical dilemma. It's problematic. I am not the Anton LaVey of this circus.

But anyway, FUCKING HELL, here it is! Or, it's one of them. *La Salpetriere* revisited. By tourists. That's what I'm calling it, the tour, or this leg of it, in which we take the funnel at a good clip into the deep basement, the old severe division. Just a quick dip to speed your trip. Something to get you started.

Still, it is very dark down here, so each exhibit must be lamp-lit. You couldn't make this stuff up. I mean, you could, but any scenario you can think of is a meme already. In the original sense. Consider the Purgative Cure, now a popular fetish, which retains the medieval flourishes. It is not so much over-determined as derivative in this instance. All the inessentials boiled off to a stagnant base of vitreous humour and bone meal.

We call these ghosts the floaters. This is someone's daughter. Sorry about that, but I've always thought if you can see look is good advice. If not, then close your eyes and just start weeping. Either way, this is really happening. This is already scripted. Just don't shoot the tour guide. That's not so much a disclaimer as begging.

I mean whose soul are we talking about anyway? I didn't start this fire. Neither did you, I'm sure, even though we're getting warm off of it. So, what's with all the talk of guilt and shame and breakaway tunnels?

Nothing's free. Never has been. Everything needs a financial engine. The Virginia Tobacco brides are on the auction block with Irish boys and African slaves. In fact, reprise all manner of fetters, stocks and scolds' bridles. A 4chan/b thread salivates at the aesthetics of this, except I can't access the graphics, being unvetted. Typically, there is no need for vetting. The contents are right there on the surface. There is nothing to be fetched up. It's all free range and open air now. It's all backrooms and dungeons. Suspension rigs and drill bits pivoting. It's all one whack and you're out. It's a lot of high-speed whacking into oblivion.

If it makes you feel better, we've set up a stall where a trepanning will tap your demons and drain them through a spigot, like maple syrup. Wear your bone as a chaser. This is also where the Aztec death whistle comes in. That screeching has served a variety of purposes from human sacrifice rituals to warfare, and now here. It's very authentic in the original sense, though we're a bit sketchy on the details. Well it's not meant to be PLEASANT. It's a bloody asylum isn't it? Think horror. Think mockumentary where the director is up on charges for missing crew members:"

"I am thinking horror," says Lucy A. "I'm especially concerned about that sharp turn, after which the uncanny blurs to splattered gore. It's open season and no one is accountable to any authority; your only allegiance to shock doctrine. After 9-11, there is a sharp spike in non-elective surgeries alongside a salon of laboratories opening up to explore the limits of inhumanity in cinema."

"Hmm, well you might be surprised who the audience is for this. If it was just restricted to sensory-addicted college kids, you could dismiss it as some sort of fad, this revival. Then you could put a lid on it. But we've tapped the real housewives demographic, just look at the stats, and once you do that, you're a fount of streaming potential. Skip the other one and go straight to Spinoza. His Red Brigade's kill list was never confirmed. Or look at the traffic. The main entry is clogged on a Sunday afternoon, as if someone put a cork in it. This does make it hard for the crew to maneuver. But business is good; and that's the arbiter. Look who we have for a mascot."

"That's what I'd wanted to talk to you about, actually." Lucy drops a thick packet of news clippings at his feet. Reports of missing persons, most of them homeless folks and prostitutes. About what happens when you remove the deathless portion of the death wish? About what is really happening here when there is so much guilt built up, and so relentlessly, that it's a machine needing a sacrifice, a very real ghost? Just to try to preserve, or is it to destroy, empathy?

Crepitus exhales exaggeratedly, with rasping and wheezing.

"With that, I've lost my flow, mid-tour. I suppose I'd left myself vulnerable to these interruptions with my open-door policy. In any case, we'll have to tie a bow in it there because I need to do a quick wardrobe change before meeting with this very demanding patient. Yes, I know, blame it on her BPD, baby. Because despite being reformed, this new ward is not in fact free from the grips of her parasitic sister, still rattling her chains in the cellar.

In any case, you will have to see yourselves out. If you can. But it's not as easy going up. It's not as easy going in reverse. Getting better instead of worse.

And should you at any time find yourself on the wrong side of the glass, where you can only sense that something is out there, something that means you some harm, but with all its intentions folded up inside as tripe, you can mount no defense from that position as I keep saying. You might as well pray for it at that point, the quickening. That's right, I said prey."

"That's exactly how I feel when Blue Eye says I'm so small like a girl," Lucy worries. "As if I'd swallowed the wrong pill, and then he tries to fatten me up with some condensed milk."

"Blue Eye is one of our permanent wards," Crepitus explains to the tourists who are shuffling out. "Though he is permitted some exercise time in yard, I assure you." "That's where we met of course," Lucy continues. "He specifically wanted to know if I liked my involuntary confinement. And then afterward, absently walked off and said just 'ground hamburger'. It made no sense because he had already prepared 'the pig' for the spit, as he called it. At which point, you should stop talking about meat."

"Ground hamburger? That is odd," Crepitus says, perplexed. "Blue Eye typically has more exotic tastes. You'll hear, should you return for my next module! He's one of our underground stars, featured in our reenactment of The Drowning Chamber. This ultimate test of true hysteria. Will she swim, or will she drown? It's an interesting development indeed that he should be one of Lucy's suitors."

"I wish you wouldn't call them suitors." Lucy continues to look worried. "It all has a very 'Silence of the Lambs' feel already. At any moment, I expect you to break into that see-saw cadence as a form of dark humour. It's either that or 'American Psycho'–his aura. Like when we were in queue for our C2 admixture and he rubbed his semi up against me. It was right after I'd confessed to being terrified he meant to eat me. He did immediately apologize, but on the grounds that it transgressed some etiquette for standing in line. It seemed the equivalent of handing me a business card."

"Well you can't very well complain, Lucy, when you said you prefer men with attachment blankness. And this seems a perfect example of your habit of misattributing ambient aggression as meant for you."

"But is it very ambient to say, when we're nearing that same sharp turn, 'Oh, by the way, right before I picked you up, I got a full tank of gas?' And while sharpening a knife, 'Would you like to go to burning man'? This . . . suitor. . .who wants no emotional connection, and seems incapable of it, suddenly wants to take me across a border. I'm not crossing any borders, not willingly. It didn't matter though, because then he said abruptly, "I'm going to change my story," and indicated his Band-aid. He had cut himself badly somehow and there was blood all over. But how can a Band-aid be a story?

He knows that's a recurring refrain. And it's not the only one. A lot of them say things like, "I know how to survive in any environment and I know how to start a fire from nothing, and 90 percent of all people who say they can actually can't, and while holding up dead animals in their profiles."

"Many of what?"

"My suitors who are sizing me up. And you want to ask them when are they going to be in a survivalist scenario? Is it in a forest? It is, isn't it? And Burning Man is something else."

"Ugh, not you too? Please tell me you're not referring to that irritating Alex Jones tape?"

"Well, Sid says it's somewhere on your extended grounds. The cremation I mean. And I've seen myself there's a stead light burning."

SUSPECT M

"Well then, I'm sure he's also been telling you about the experiments. And how he thinks himself a patsy. He hasn't tried to sell you some medicinal THC has he? He's obsessed about a subplot concerning Big Pharma and has had some success getting patients to refuse their meds. You need to tell me if that happens."

"What I feel is that there is something in this facility compelling me to associate with your most dangerous patients. Almost as if it's unavoidable. Like a set-up."

"Indeed, I had been observing your interactions along the fourth wall. And, I can tell by your pallor that you had a near brush. You must report these if we are to build trust. Quid pro quo, Lucy, quid pro quo."

"Well, the brush was with Sid's associate, the one they call The Handler–who is connected."

"You think they're a pair, then? Like partners? I'd suspected as much. And what did his associate say that has you so spooked?"

"Well, he told everyone to leave the area except Sid and me. Then he gave me an impromptu screening of a Serbian film, except lower-budget, and set in Brazil, just the severing near the end, and said, 'It's called "No Pussy Pass". Women who act tough here suffer the same consequences as men.' And since then, I've heard him many times repeat that phrase to Sid, paired with an ultra-violent film clip."

"'No Pussy Pass'? That is unusual. What then?"

"Then, he called me a taxi back to my room. Or, you might say 'summoned' because the driver was an associate too. And he'd obviously been in some drug experiments because his eyes were glazed as crackle and he was weaving into oncoming traffic to some soul-snuffing black metal and saying 'I could tell you stories. I could tell you stories.' Repeating that."

"And then what happened?"

"And then he said, 'I could tell you stories about a group of cabbies who like to take women to off-grid areas where they get lost.' He then said this was bad for business. Bad for business! It's that odd etiquette again, that civility where empathy should be. I thought, this is it, this is the set-up, finally, where you're out on a cliff face. The scenario where they're about to drop the shovel.

"And then?"

"And then he drove me to my room."

"Right, of course, because you're here."

"Am I? Because I feel changed."

"Well, only insofar as you seem to be identified with a dead person. So, don't be too curious."

"But I can't help but wonder what's on the other side of all the abutments that I can only sense. In which case, it might be better if it was staged and right out in the open for everyone to see – documented."

"Yes! That's why we have the trauma reenactments. And to make good use of our patients' propensities for being lying actresses."

"Lying? Is that what you meant by my 'mock delusional act.' Do I still seem mock to you? I mean, am I a very bad actor?"

"No, you're believable. But the real question is, am I? Do you believe that I possess any special knowledge about your case? It's very important that you do. I'd like to do a little test. Remember that the Yard is full of eyes and I already know the answer to the question I'm asking."

SUSPECT M

"Alright."

"Now then, tell me Lucy, Sid said something to you before you left in the taxi, under his breath. What was it?"

"He said, 'I'll try to keep you safe.'"

***

BLUE EYE/THE MECHANIC BEING DEAD OR AT LEAST DEPRESSING

"Freud thought the aim of repetition was to gain mastery. But clinical experience shows this rarely happens. Instead, repetition causes further suffering. This seems to be the true goal of a certain self-destructive type of patient. But what's absolutely crucial here, in terms of distinction is that in the behavioral reenactment of trauma, the self may play the role of either victim or victimizer."
– Bessel Van der Kolk, *Traumatic Stress*

As promised, Crepitus is leading a contingent of control specialists on a tour of an underground modus of the facility, the Drowning Chamber. Part of the unsavory business, conducted in the bowels of tunnel and cell that nonetheless financed the rest. As usual, he is accompanied by film students and his very demanding patient, Lucy. Just because she's pretty much always there. She's an omnipresence, really. All of them are huddled together on a light industrial trolley with Crepitus at the helm. Todd Terje's remix of "For Your Love" plays them in.

Crepitus releases the brake, causing a brief rattle of metalcore to override the disco. There is some sparking as the trolley slips wheel over track by force of momentum. The whole atmosphere has a peculiar gravity, despite certain incongruities. The entry through rubberized flaps resembling those of a fun house into a mucosal tube that seemed to be breathing. A succession of dangling insects and others are stuck to Icke's fly trap tongue, in the grips of a thing, an it, straining. Some protest art, administered by the Chamber's only permanent resident, Blue Eye. Embellishments of a childish imagination slapped as pastiche onto sweating walls; and these painted over so many times as to form a yellow cake, signed with the narcissist's dictum in cool blue. "I get what I want, and what I can't get I don't want." You can only assume it's the reason for all the repainting, and something to do with the moisture maybe.

"What makes a funhouse scary?" Lucy asks. "I mean, what is someone else's funhouse?"

Ignoring her, Crepitus flicks on the mic, which picks up his rasping as static. The subgrade air doesn't agree with him. He hauls himself up before the crowd and puts on his best tour guide mask.

"Greetings fellow physicians, and everyone. You are now entering the Chamber rotation. This is the narcissist's intermittent reinforcement schedule that is essential to our basic conditioning. It goes round and round and round and round and clearly, it's some sort of cylinder that has been jerry-rigged with an upended colander for the draining. It functions as a life-sized scold, with close-set iron bars that lift and lower on a hinge of a jaw, its captive secured within. Or without, on the other side is the ocean. It's unmitigated bliss, a reunion with your undead mother, it's terrifying."

"The scold is a mirror punishment," one of the control specialists interjects.

"Yes, [cough] whereas this lead up is only 14 feet in diameter at its maximum, so if you had any claustrophobia this would not be good for you, not even in the first instance. Consider that a warning. This is doubly true of the system of slotted shelves that drop at odd intervals, the rotator, the tickler, and the vacuum suck, after which you are carried off set. And, there are some others but, in any case, something, maybe not a gavel, but something, will drop. It will be a surprise. I can assure you its primary resident knows all there is to know about the waiting game."

"But let us remember," says the specialist, who unlike Crepitus has retained an air of dignified authority, "that his narcissism, while predominant, also tends to its opposite: an overwhelming sense of worthlessness which the patient will go to extreme lengths to avoid. This effort will ultimately involve you should you become part of his supply (which is never enough). Yes, understandably, he would rather you serve as a receptacle, a very bad receptacle, for what is intolerable in himself, which he might at some point choose to excise outright."

"So keep all limbs inside the trolley!" Crepitus shouts. "And no, this is not the part where it gets better instead of worse. We are in the decline. Think 'Cannibale Ferox'. That's a supplement we're promoting in tandem to this episode, which is already scripted, so nobody shoot the charming charlatan. It has 450 mg of caffeine and you take it right before you hit the wall if you want to simulate an authentic experience. Yes, we are in the realm of addiction. I'm a test case; I get a stipend. It's voyeurism that has nearly four dimensions. I mean, it's very close, noses pressed to the window, that sort of stuff. But nobody tell the actress; we want her fear to look realist. And nobody tell the cow. And nobody talk about the elephant in those experiments. Nothing has ever been electrified here, poor wretch."

The unit director cues a sweep of the background. A series of figures projected on canvass. It's a forest, wallpaper of a forest, and in the forefront are shadowy figures prancing with a voiceover by Crepitus, his breath now labored with rales and rasping.

"We are now nearing the Chamber's only permanent resident, Blue Eye. He's the South African cigarette smuggler whose heart is an ice pick, and incidentally, one of Lucy's suitors."

"Machinic in nature, the mechanic being dead or at least depressing, his fist contiguous with the iron handle of pulley and chain, he grinds forward in increments, as an empty ratchet, a buzzing device extending from his other hand. He is the same one in all our videos; he never takes off his clothes. Clearly, the lights are not on, so you would like to think nobody is home, but they probably are, and you can't know what they're planning in there or how it concerns you.

Sometimes, they get a kick out of telling you. And if they ever do that, believe them."

"Yes, such as when he promised to 'cook me up a killer meal,'" says Lucy.

"Except he didn't do that, did he? Because you're still here."

"No, we went to a restaurant instead, where, at one point, after scanning the menu he said, "This is no good; I need meat." And then, right after, sizing me up, "But you're so small, like a girl.""

"In any case," Crepitus continues his spiel, "when you are with him, you are alone in the room. Not really. But just due to his heart being an ice pick, which is necessary if he is to kill empathy. It will be in himself first, and then everyone else. He needn't do it serially to be effective. He needn't be a Nazi. We're not writing a Steig Larson novel. I will not make a pun about overkill. I will not make a pun about overkill. We don't buy our jokes that cheap here. Never mind the cutbacks. Never mind all the belts that need tightening. Never mind the episode called the 'Girl in the Cellar'.

No. The Cannibal Ferox are the terminal patients of the severe ward who are post-humans of no history, so the past is engorged on itself. Slow spiral of intestinal worm. Nightmarish drift down river. Corpus of the eerily familiar. The impression of teeth, a finger with last night's polish still on it. Still it's important to preserve the hair and nails, for obvious reasons.

And, as is clear by the graffiti, our star patient regards himself with a certain profundity, having been raised amongst indigenous factions that pulled off this cultural mastication with a conviction, so that when they said 'No, we are not the barbarians here,' but pointed instead to the bloody edifice, you were inclined to believe them.

At base, his Chamber is a playpen. And what we have here is a spoiled infant modeling a dada who, likewise, had the instinctual renunciation of a child with a biting problem. Even his therapy sucks Pablum. Albeit through a straw with a rifling sound."

Sensing an audience, Blue Eye pulls his thumb from his latest plumb and says, "See who's a good boy; you can love me again. Also, I'm not just a plumber. I built this whole thing." He grins pearly white.

"Will you look at those teeth," Crepitus remarks. "Still. You will find him handsome at first. People do, people like you. As you can see, he's square-jawed and fit, a romantic walk off a savanna cliff. That's the ad, the hook in the upper lip. Better than the ad is the trip. You will follow him, follow him wherever he may go, at a clip, through his amphitheater rows that are razor sharp, his switch-hit of pursuit and evasion. It's heady and dreamlike, right up until the stun. Then it's a downward drag into suffocating vacuum. His sinkhole emptiness. He doesn't care too much, unlike you. He knows what he's doing; that's unlike you too. So Takyon, you're in. His second location. No Love. And you are either suffocating or drowning. Take your ice pick and like it."

The camera dials in as Blue Eye delivers his line with the detached air of a fellow scientist. "Notice how at this point she will actually dissociate." The shot pans to the suspended figure, up on the wall in reverb. "I . . . want . . . to die," she gurgles between convulsions, tipping into oblivion.

"I predict that very soon he will simply lop her off," Crepitus comments.

"You mean dump her," says Lucy.

"Yes, and with her his feelings of impotence and homicidal jealousy. But, do I detect some enmity Lucy?"

"Yes, because they all have the same lines, just slightly varied. They say things like 'I'm a spoiled child' and 'I will win, I always do.' And when we had our palms read in the lobby your mystic said, 'The man who lives in the chamber has demons and is a Tiger; whereas, she said I'm a Monkey."

"Well," he immediately quipped, "The Tiger eats the Monkey, it EATS the Monkey."

"But then I said 'Well maybe you won't win because monkeys are clever. I'll outsmart you.' Which is when he dumped me too, for Sophia."

"Yes, yes. Love only breaks up to start all over again. That saw. With the rotating teeth."

"I win. I always do," Blue Eye says in deadpan.

"Do you really? Because your face is in tatters as if you had tried to drown a cat. I'm guessing it was her. If you ever got in close, she would surely do it again."

"I prefer this really," says the one up on the wall. "I'd rather be a ghost than a swallower. And it wouldn't be as bad if you were to care. Do you love me yet, just a little bit?"

"Well this facility makes it hard to love anyone." Crepitus gives a nervous laugh. "I mean' it's sex with no hands and the stage lighting is all wrong."

"Let's just say that she's worthless now. She IS worthless now," says Blue Eye. Releasing the spring of the jaw, he launches his latest catch into the ocean. Or what is actually the facility's main drain.

"With that she's expired, poor wretch." Crepitus bows his head solemnly. "Simulation's over comrades."

***

THE PALM READER FROM THE LOBBY/A READING BETWEEN CLUE AND TAROT

"We're all going down the rabbit-hole. And that's an order."
– Steve Venright, *The End of History*

This is a visioning engine. Buzzing. The palm reader is in his anointed spot outside the lobby's gift shop. It glows psychedelic over his right shoulder in a mesmeric weave that wants you to enter its twisting pattern. A contractual oracle for guests of the asylum. He flips cards, a cross between Clue and Tarot, along his fingers and turns them up. A reading.

"We are not in the ascent yet, not here," he intones. Even as you are back in your room, here you are in an irreal world of dream and under a spell as in a true fairytale. His Lair. That's the first card. His home he has burrowed into a trap. You can still see in the threshold, the crescent of an iron hook. "Pick Your Own Retreat" it says on top. This is the prediction.

"In the coming Wolf's Age, the tree will be entirely inverted so that the canopy is all under. The one law of Do What You Will is the tyranny of total liberty become final. His rule inside is outside also, expanding, called by many names, but still most recognized by his fetid breath and spiked mange.

The Wolfsangel. The sign of a contradiction. The one that feeds you wants to eat you. You don't get there in one swallow.

It starts with a curse cast at the ceremony of your birth that fishes up your spine a crooked tree screwed into the axis of the earth. And from there, a series of fractures spidering out across a crystal plain.

The first trauma is a catastrophic disruption of the attachment system.

Do you remember? This is where they come for the children who are torn from breasts and in their place surrogates of wire and mesh, children who will nonetheless cling with desperate mouths and bellies, aching to be filled with something, pining. And the mothers, too, unhinged-like creatures, will wander throughout for days, blocking passages, causing disease, their unguent turned venomous without release, through distortion of hysteria, susceptible to further disturbances that are seismic in nature.

The second trauma is a corruption at the site of virtue and pleasure.

A funnel opens, a pucker into which his obelisk is seized and swallowed up; it bores high-speed into ever deeper and darkening tunnels. That's the primary direction of the current expansion. Down. We are going down and getting worse. We are getting more and more hidden in fixation.

Of course, there have always been secret societies, but advances in technology have made it possible for the tunnels to almost completely break away from the surface-civilization while remaining in some mode visible to everyone. Through a radiating screen.

That's how it spreads. As streaming carnivorous spores. The third trauma, where empathy is killed behind a veil of purity.

SUSPECT M

[Diorama for a later scene.]

The Wolfsangel's Lair is a Cremation of Care at the foot of the Sadist's Castle on an acreage deep in the forest. Or, what is actually a national park with contested jurisdiction and a disproportionate number of missing persons. Sophia P. is one of them.

A fortified barracks of charred leavings, his chambers are lined with clippings. Like an archive of everyone who has been to the retreat and never left, a sort of guest list.

Here the masculine is rabid, the feminine choked off, in a post-zed dead end. It's a backward-looking zed actually, nativist, where the uncanny gives way to torture porn and the elites and transgressives have all the same victims and are building a pyre in a grove where they have lured them. This fantasy is now so widespread it's become a world forum of guilt; a ritual sacrifice is needed to expunge it.

The Purgative Cure. This one is a GIF where she keeps reentering the forest and the forest keeps reentering her so that she can't breathe, her hair wound tightly in its bright fist.

It relates to the governing card. Death Wish. A collision of your personal truth and a general one. You deserve what you get. You do it to yourself. Risky lifestyle. Instrumentalized as worthless.

Still if you know anything about fairytales and spells, you know there are protective elements that you have to believe in– the first is that you are worth saving. Then, you have to persuade everyone, or enough of everyone, that you are either saint or witch enough to issue a divine command.

Here you have Evola quoting de Maistre at the moment of the curse. 'A woman can only be superior as a woman. As soon as she tries to imitate a man, she is nothing but a monkey.'

So that's you Monkey. You're the Good News. A figure card.

If you know anything about conspiracies, you know the breakaway tunnels aren't the only alternative. There are other planets you can live. They can't all be colonized and populated with slaves. That's the other direction of the current expansion, up and out. This dream is stuck. We might just have to leave it behind.

But, if you know anything about ascents, you know you have to earn them. You can't just fly out an open window. They have nets for that, set up around all the workstations. It's part of what makes this journey spiritual. It seems impossible."

***

LUCY AND SOPHIA ARE DISSOCIATED/THE HANDLER IS CONNECTED

"And Sophia cried out most exceedingly, she cried to the Light of lights, which she had seen from the beginning . . . and uttered this repentance: Save me, O Light, for evil thoughts have entered into me."
– *Pistis Sophia*, Chapter 32

And so, Lucy stayed back in her room, inside of a protective skin, as Sophia went forward and landed on a heap of sticks and dry leaves at the lip of the funnel, the curl of a fly trap, Icke the dirty old toad having run his tongue along it.

On waking, Lucy starts to protest, banging, dry thuds against reinforced wood. "This isn't a pay it forward situation. Dissociation. You can't just substitute Sophia for me and call everyone a phantom. You can't leave me here forever, identified with a dead person. I'm not the same as easier. She's just a baby. Still, they say you shouldn't feed us. We're in cages for a reason."

***

It takes a village to deliver a child into this, to help you find your right level of risk.

"And, in my 12 years as a physician on the DTES," says Mate, "I don't know of one female patient who was not sexually abused as a child or adolescent, nor a male who hadn't suffered some severe form of trauma."

Sophia was groomed over several generations, her ancestors driven from the fertile plains, their herds culled, and reservoirs drained, until the knock at the door. "I've come for your prettiest daughter," he says, as in a true fairytale. It's the one where he comes for the children and plays them outside, repeated over centuries for some reason.

When Sophia was a child they'd take one look at her and offer her candy. They'd lightly touch her shoulder to establish a field of propriety. As a teen, they grabbed her in the shelter line. A layer of protectors gathered round her. But nothing's free. She hadn't had her own home since aging out at 16 unless you count her cell. She was 22 when Lucy first met her. By then, she was managed by a team. The push out started in grade one, the vector she is still on, on the outskirts of a universe much like this one.

He came for Sophia in starts, a pattern revving up. At one point, their tracks disappeared into damp woods, that rivet.

Why, at other points, is there only one set of footprints?

"That's when he carried her," comes the answer. It seems on behalf of a conspiracy rising up against them as self-hatred. His death drive turned inward. His obelisk shifting into gear.

He first spots Sophia in the mall sitting round a table with friends. Their gestures are broad and animated as she shrinks into herself, arms hiding her chest, not aloof but insecure. The wrong haircut, the wrong clothes, a backpack holding everything she owns. All the tells.

He first spots Sophia in the atrium with a friend. She is taller by nearly a head and manikin thin. With arms linked, they float past him.

An awkward bird, he thinks, with long legs that are wish bones, twigs. He could star her in a Serbian film, but lower budget and set in Brazil. A carrier pigeon on the outs with a drug cartel.

As if catching a scent, he snatches up his coffee cup and follows them out, slowing his pace to lag a ways behind as they all bear down on the ribbons of highway that stretch into the Broadway night.

He first spots Sophia talking to a guard. She's explaining why she sleeps out in the open under the lights. "Well, what do you want me to do about it? I can't exactly unrape you, can I?" he says and moves her along.

He first spots Sophia on the roadside. With no bus service, she's hitching in. He pulls up slightly ahead of where she stands. Looking straight ahead he just says, "Lift?"

***

SID M. IS AN EXPERT IN ALL THEIR PROGRAMS

"It's got the same signature as the asylum's DID experiments," says Sid, who has joined Lucy in the lobby. A Todd Terje extended version of "Superstition" surrounds them. "All of us have been put through some mind control regimen to simulate the intermittent conditioning of the narcissistic parasite. This is often started in infancy. They get you to bind emotionally to one adult person, a surrogate parent, who treats you lovingly. That prepares the necessary defenseless state of felt safety for the first fracture to be introduced. For this, you are mistreated by your very same beloved, subjected to inappropriate behavior, character assassination, sexual abuse, even torture, all tactics that, paired with the loving treatment, trigger a protective mechanism in the brain. Confronted by irreconcilable realities, the pain and its source get split off or dissociated, walled off as an internal entity. Almost like an organ, a hostile transplant, it stays unassimilated and often unremembered. Until triggered, that is. The adult then renews the loving treatment, which tightens the amnesia."

"It reminds me of a scene that replays in my head," Lucy reminisces. It involves myself and an older female. The two of us are sitting on a bed with her hugged in behind rolling curlers up into my hair. Her powdery perfume cuts into my throat. She is trying to make me into a little doll, so we match better. Me and this woman they call whore in the streets, whose windows they smash because she's strange and has too many boyfriends. While curling my hair she recites the same story again and again with slight variation, about a willful girl called Little Red who disappears. The ending went something like this.

"Then one day, it happened. The girl put aside her mother's warnings and gave in to her foolish desire. In the low sun of late afternoon, her feet danced on pavement, her long shadow running on the shapes of the road, its rough and empty passage. And as her feet first touched the dark stirrings that inwardly strung shrouds between trunks, she was gone."

"'So be a good girl even in your dreams'," she would say. "'And don't cut through the park to school because Threinen the child killer waits there. And don't open the cellar door because a stranger once hung himself beneath your floor boards. Also, it's cold and damp and prone to aggressive branching and polyphonic wheezing'."

Just like here, they send an officer to protect us and instead of getting better we get worse. It's clear in the scene that they mean me to become her. She's the original mother."

"That definitely sounds like an implant," Sid nods. "Those usually have some repressed elements, a mode of self-protection that can become maladaptive. But maladaptive for who is the question. The aim of the program is to fragment the mind, to split the personality repeatedly and deliberately, with each personality fragment, also called an alter, then amenable to further programming.

Conceivably a single sub can possess within themselves thousands of alters, though each of them usually believes it's the only one and knows nothing about the existence of the rest.

You and Sophia are from project Kitten, which involves a lot of licking and purring and nuzzling. And you're also part Carrier Pigeon, like me, a sort of recording-transmitting device, a projector, with scenes that play like a film across your face. And you're a third thing, unintended I think, possibly some sort of switch. I can tell you more about switches and keys and triggers later. But that's unlike Sophia. In fact, the two of you are now at almost opposite ends of a trait. While she's been driven to the outermost depths, you can barely leave your room."

"Because I'm afraid."

"Well, you don't want to ignore that impulse to flee. That's a Dorothy trigger, the Scare Crow trying to warn you about something you can't see, such as intentions, auras, floaters. Crepitus says the asylum is for the Healing of Souls, but no one knows what happens to people once they leave. How do we know is even a real doctor?"

"Not a real doctor," Lucy repeats.

***

"The Handler said if I don't want to go to dinner he has 3.9 acres where he likes to entertain," she continues. "I'm curious what that is. And why a patient would have their own acreage on asylum grounds."

"I told you he's connected. But remember what the dream says. A curious girl is a sin, with consequences."

"But you must know what goes on there; he's your friend."

SUSPECT M

"We're associates, there's a difference. I've never been to any of his parties."

"I find that hard to believe."

"Well, it's true. And you shouldn't speak to him directly. You should go through me."

"But he invited me."

"Well, be careful then. There's a hierarchy and he's closer to the Great Animator. You know that gesture they make with their thumb and forefinger? It means 'we're going to link up.' The whole purpose of the love cure if you think about it. All of us here are pining for our other half. But not like a twin, more like two hemispheres."

"And when we come together, maybe that's the end of our therapy and we get released? Who is the Great Animator?"

"It's hard to say exactly because everything is inverting. But he has the head of an owl and the obelisk of a bull."

"I've felt that way too, that we're in the upside-down. Crepitus says that the One Law of 'do what you will' is a law of love and freedom. But whose freedom are we talking about exactly, when there are so many patients in cages and patrols around our edges? And Blue Eye, the star patient, lives almost entirely underground."

"Yes, and not only that. He's clearly a Golden Boy/Lady Killer type with his oceanic blue eye and hot sand hair."

"But you seem to think the Handler might mean me some harm, that his Pick Ur Own Retreat is a trap."

"No, he's not stupid, you're protected. Not from everything obviously. But it says right on your profile you have an advanced degree. Still, it's a secret society of some kind. 'Eyes Wide Shut', but lower tier, a rustic B & B."

"That's not very secret, actually."

"It's a cover. And they might pretend you're going one place then they take you somewhere else. Watch yourself."

"There it is again, that aura of threat, and emanating from you."

"It's just that there are a lot of creeps out there and you never know when someone might get a bad idea."

"It was creepy of him to scare me with that clip. And to say it was a Serbian film when it was clearly lower budget and set in Brazil and about a woman on the outs with a drug cartel."

"The only drug cartel is Big Pharma. They have a strangle hold on the asylum. He just wanted to see if you'd report it. There's a code"

"A code? But then why did he say 'No Pussy Pass'?"

"'No Pussy Pass' is the name of a breakaway tunnel. He was trying to warn you. Actually, we should go for a walk in the garden. I want to show you something and the yard has too many eyes."

"Is this the part where you take me somewhere else?"

***

[In an especially neglected part of the garden. Sound of distant batons slapping]

"You won't like this part," Sid whispers. "It's from the tapes of a penal guard who once worked here, who quit the force and sued them for obstructing his progress on the missing person's file. He goes by the name Romeo."

Sid turns on the tape.

"This is K. T. Romeo>" The audio labours and crackles. "My speculations on some found footage of a crime scene containing Sophia P.'s residual energy. Copy that."

"It cuts off right before the film students become a skeleton crew. It explains how you could have seen Sophia in three figurations when entering the facility, but then also first met her on the Broadway nights only moments before she disappeared into an unmarked vehicle.

It implies circularity. One time. Realities stacked as thinly shaved pastrami re-laminated. It's at least true that once someone is missing and behind dark-tinted glass they could also be anywhere else. She disappears and reappears and reappears again, doomed between apparition and flesh. She has over a million hits.

What do I mean by flesh? It's her vomit isn't it? Also, that idea of the soul being captured isn't mere superstition. It's a leap that happens under circumstances of severe trauma. She's actually in the partition–like Tympana–vibrating. She's vibrating. It's similar to what the ancients called limbo.

You can tell by the architectural detail it has a religious significance, and by the smudges it signals taboo. We're the first generation to leave left-handed fingerprints. Her file is the dirtiest I've seen, but otherwise typical of this medieval revival we're experiencing. All the instruments are stuck. An eternity collar staked to a chain in a stone subbasement that could be anywhere. A scalpel that looks like a machete or wheat thresher. Her figure ballooned out in a translucent blouse of skin then pulled taught over a rack of ribs. They like it brute and distorted. Thick-thin, I believe they call it. What was it the reformed French Israeli said about love with no hands? It's whatever the viewer finds exciting. Do they want to see you beg and cry? Do they want it to look realist? Nobody tell the actress.

While we don't know the exact location, we can make out the etching behind her in chalky white. The Purgative Cure. She's clearly somewhere in the asylum."

Sid shuts it off. "Tell me that isn't damning evidence against Crepitus and this facility, of his trauma reenactments and his basement tours? He says they're a simulation, but then winks to the camera. He's exploiting the idea that you can never be sure. And what about the film students from Whileawayan Liberal U? They actually advertise that they're making a paranormal documentary in which the subject lies a lot. They're mocking us, their critics."

***

THE GIRL IN THE CELLAR/UNTO YOU A MONKEY IS BORN

"At last this odious offspring, thine own begotten, breaking violent way, tore through my entrails, that, with fear and pain . . . all my nether shape thus grew transformed."
– John Milton, *Paradise Lost*

"Those who feel me near pull the blinds and change their minds."
– David Bowie, "Cat People/Putting Out Fire"

This was before Lucy was christened by suggestion of anti-woman during the Trials of Ghomeshi. "Don't stick your cigar in crazy," the commentator said as he and his teddy bear got off. That poisoned dart marked his accuser, another Lucy, and polluted the canal around her, the spot of a woman's baptism in her third manifestation, whose creator said, on hearing the caution to this victim of female spite "That's perfect, really." Presto. Another loose saint.

Monkey was before that, before before that, when Lucy was still a girl on the verge living with her god-mother in some neglected garden or other, for the most part the same one there is now, surrounded by a fringe of grey buildings.

It was in response to an external catalyst, a word, *Hairlip*, that issued along her god-mother's tongue and slithered into a crevice of her rib. Heat expanding in a fluid sac. A foaming spiral of pin-pricked tissue in a half-life of distorted unbirth. It's good to know how I look, thought Lucy, at least when fully formed.

And there it was where it wasn't before, a cleft lip, a furred mug, confirmed by her god-mother's mirror, a special mirror between the way things seem and the way things are. The difference was the mystery, a funnel pulling in everything. Lucy was the fault at its insecure center, under edging suspicion that she was not really just a girl, but also something sinister, she patrolled her own features.

At the very least the she was the enemy of perfect. A wisp of grey drizzle ruining. Loose debris hit her in passing. Denied the small "no" of a child, the mere sight of her kicked up sparks she feared and therefore brought upon herself. Ingested. Believed. And every fear a wish and every wish a prayer.

As charge turned to flesh, pick and cut became thoughts. Still an apparent nine-year-old girl, but now tending a bit wild. Just a hairline run of blood vessel along inward curve of a lid, in fluid. Translucent and blind, toothless feeding, in part from living so near a grey forest.

In grave need of a protector and unable to secure one. She passed between impersonal caretakers, held at a distance. What does that say? That she really was something dreadful. Not just a girl, but also something else sinister. A hidden minefield or a switch no one wanted to go off on their watch.

Even when your prayer is finally answered, it's often not how you expected. A cloud of spores moving in like an animal through low mist. The master's voice his mastiff's steel, the law in every sense. What he could want with them she can't fathom at first. "Can't he see we're not right?", she asked no one in particular.

SUSPECT M

"He's not right," welled up the answer.

This beast was large and spread out everywhere, with smell that permeated thick like zoo, leavings of coarse dark hair, loud and grunting from the bedroom, he roamed naked and feral without regard for barriers.

She moved her nights underground and curled into the husk of a shelter, the remains of an earlier threat, unnamed and now forgotten. Not bombs, too fragile. An outer wall of mattresses propped against bookshelves, made more sturdy by a hoard of instant foods, stubbed candles, and C cells. And piles of stale books, her god-mother's.

One was about a girl like her, only slightly older. Justine. "Virtue" it said on the cover. Buried under a stack of others it confirmed the governing order. Prepared it, really. The right to do with children as you wish. And who would contest it? Not the crippled alloys of Virtue who were cleaved against trees and pursued into cellars.

What a world! It might be better to tuck yourself into a seam in which to imagine and dream until it was all over.

She dragged over a metal cot and bundled blankets to cushion the springs and in roots of inverted canopy, swirls of bright tapestry, clung to the rungs of its ceiling.

As above, so it is below. Mushrooms bent in a wicked wind. Bitter morsels full of sin. Prickly weave of egg sack. Mermaid's purse and salt chimera. Tumbling over creases, rifts, embankments that were almost alive. They shed a pulsation along her.

The gentle rocking of a lullaby. Familiar playground tonality, but with deeper undertow. Lips crackling at the edge of hearing. Something violent inward stirring.

A tug, cloying as a hangnail broadening. Through a bundle of nerve fibers flourishing. Cramping. Down and out in parietal branching. Her ribcage yanked down in sudden contraction., "What does bleed mean?" Lucy asked.

"It means you're ready," the voice said, so certain.

Heat mounting in her head. A small red flame eating sulfur. The report of chemical jolts over the node, dead-center in the slowest somersault. A ripple of tiny convulsions. Soft clouded sensation of necessity. Something ingested being purged. "Virtue," it said on the cover.

A slick black mange is crowning, oily head moored to billowing substrate. Folded tripe. The night sky. A tap opening. Is it with blood or water to tear the pearly white?

Slits narrowing in cranial darkness peer out. Come on! Sharp teeth at odd angles glint steel. Go out! A bonnet of shadow retracts. A glimpse of the right supraorbital notch in green light. A clipped bark.

Monkey.

She strains her waxen mask, blinks gummy eyes and, finding the right purchase of her freedom, swallows poison , rakes the claw of a can-opener from pubis to sternum and drips a tell-tale trail to the welfare reception.

"Silly worker, Monkey's not 'a monkey'," she will say to ashen faces, not so accustomed as you might think. Neither is anything necessarily what it seems. Not even a girl who could be vessel for some ancient vampire or savior.

But that was before before the Trials; and we are now after. Monkey is now long in the tooth, her aversive power greatly diminished, in retrograde. Not very libidinal. That may be why Lucy has returned to this earlier period of the encroachments. She'd let her guard down and the wrong motif crept in. Or she wished for the wrong thing, which when it arrives, is often not as

SUSPECT M

you expected. Plus, it's all very cyclical. Love only breaks up to start all over again. That funnel. That rotating saw with its teeth at all the exits. This borderline facility tilting on its axis.

* * *

IT'S A VIRTUAL PENAL STATE/IT IS NOT GOING TO PROTECT YOU

"Forgive me. I'm guilty. I'm bad. I'm wrong. . . I've never done anything bad. I'm not a bad person. . . I am Nancy Angelo. I'm an artist. I'm a nun of my own design."
– Alexandra Juhasz, "Bad Girls Come and Go, but a Lying Girl Can Never Be Fenced In" in *Feminism and Documentary*

"'A LYING GIRL CAN NEVER BE FENCED IN.' That's what the film students say. Or well, everybody says we malinger; but to not be fenced in seems a good idea. To not come and go.

Because just as there are greater insanities than the ones said to originate in people, there are also greater lies. To the extent these emanate from me, it is only that I have never been a very bad girl, but a covert girl. That's a very different mode of being that lends itself to a very different self-protection if I'm being honest as to the nature of my resistance, which I am. If I'm being honest about the nature of my anxiety and compulsion.

In fact, to really feel okay here, to tolerate it, I think I'd have to seize his obelisk and run the whole thing. But then, there's the old problem of using the master's tool. You become him. And in this case, he's a bit of a sadist, isn't he?

SUSPECT M

Okay, so. . . globally replace my ultra-private confessionals to a former patient turned penal guard, strapped into an e-cubicle with me like a priestly society of a cross encompassing the world.

SORRY, sounding board.

I am that way. Committed. Really believing in something. Religiously submitting my complaints before absentee authority to protect me. Wishing and hoping and waiting and praying and nobody answering. Though, as you will soon see, slowly regaining the clarity of my voice from all the attempts to gag and mute and suffocate me, and no longer speaking like a stilted Victorian.

Soon you will realize the revenge-reversal of what you think my recovery is supposed to entail. So-called audiences. Lucy the fallen saint. The bad witness. Not the brightest star in the galaxy, but still with her own documentary.

No, that is not *in public*. Or it better not be. A two-way mirror before a darkened audience, lit up, is my least favorite type of mirror. Say something! Just kidding. But that's what confinement means. Keeping your symptoms within a treatable range of circumscribed boxes, i.e., your room, or other people's rooms. I don't know why. What's fear again?

I don't have any real profile, but my virtual one says 'No sexting plz, just politics and religion.' That part's true.

You might be surprised how many respondents. I am. Just given my un-pristine face and nearly unbearable personality. Although they are perhaps not fully appreciative yet.

First surveys. What do you think of SJW's who don't need you to open their door, but then when they're working on their car and you don't help, call you inconsiderate asshole? What do you think of sluts who wear underwear in public, and pant suits, and won't sleep with you? What do you think of our Nancy-boy prime minister? What do you think of 51 fluids under the contortionist rainbow? What do you think of skin and shapes and hand gestures? What do you think of THOTS that are really scantily dressed local police monitoring your online hate speech? Do you add them anyway because they're hot; and does it ever bother you that you're, well, in front of cops? What do you think of homeless zealots trying to force their conspicuous lifestyles down your children's throats when all they want to do is see the new 'Star Wars'?

Yes, so that's all very encouraging.

In other good news, I have, so far, passed all the witches-tests designed to expose my fakery and exorcisms. Have you? My catalogue of abuse. My trials and tormenters. My plagues. My jaw, outlined in pitter-patter of what are they? Like venom-filled boils franchising unto the outermost extremities. Even my room isn't safe and quarantined. Seal all the leaks in double plastic. Set fire to the bed and poison everything. Some people are just more allergic to plagues.

All for straying from the family hearth. But still not enough to break my spiritual quest. In this I am encouraged by the story of a young Sophia P., sent here for the crime of self-emanating.

That's the rumor circulating–that we make the best lay analysts. You think I'm the one who decided that's the crux of my affliction? Clearly, you have not been paying attention. It's always the site of corruption. Look it up. It's very original. It's not just me; it's you. It's every time Sophia performs those poses ending in the promise of a new world, or even if you were to click on her in the small death-well that steals a little of her power. It just does.

SUSPECT M

What do you want to do? Pretend that's not who's in here? Neglected house wives with the morals of prostitutes, who like men? Did I say that? Asking for a friend. And do you know who else? Actual prostitutes. Sex survivalists. Also, frigids, ageds, noncompliants, unnurturants, drug-addled addicts, rambling politico witches. Most in very ashamed self-loathing. But yes, I'm sure you can add to that Penal State and your pill pushing White Veil Order of Goodie Nurses still doing all your caring work and decency for you.

That's right. In shifts of crisp uniforms, ever since this asylum began working hand-in . . . well, it's some sort of sterile latex prophylaxis against the feminine dregs, as one of the alien doctors called us. FALLEN WOMEN ARE NOT GOOD REPRESENTATIVES OF THE REST OF WOMEN. That's what unredeemable means.

I know what you're going to say is if you were me you'd choose alone and lonely. Well what a noble and moral calling. Except you aren't are you? Or well. If you are then affinity is my favorite esoteric symbol."

***

OUT IN THE YARD/ THE PENAL GUARD

"Although the need for nurturance cannot be entirely replaced by coitus, we often see overwhelming sexual desire in undernourished individuals."
– Sabina Spielrein, *Destruction as the Cause of Coming into Being*

At some point, you get the sense that dating is a cover, a floating stage set. He drives you up to the ridge of the strip, pries her fingers from his coat, and says, "Take responsibility for YOURSELF." In the end, a reptilian society. He doesn't matter anymore as a person. Seal the body up as a crypt. Scales erupt in a ligature of armour split black. He's the penal guard out in the yard of an institution. If he ever was something else, a patient or comrade, no one remembers. There's a whole force of him perched on top a secret store of ammo. A mere tap on the floor of the inner ward, sets of lips flutter to the surface to feed him. Incandescent paint slathering against glass. Red batons of lacquered wood spring up along her perimeter, impinging.

"It's all about boundaries, this policing function," he dins into the conditioned air. His lecture to the new cadets. Who defines them, what gets in and out. "And as a borderline facility, ours are notoriously bad, porous as a sieve of code-blue violations. Terrible! That's the press if you read it.

Be especially wary of the sycophants [gripping Lucy's forearm in his rough paw]. These parasites will want to turn your dealings into a capital-R Relationship; they have all manner of tricks to pull you in and garner false sympathy. Especially when you're trying to eject them from the Yard; they'll stick to you like suckerfish [tipping his third eye toward at her]. Yes, you dear are the drain on all this to be stopped, by tourniquet if necessary.

So, be sure to keep them at arms-length to protect the integrity of the institution. These boundaries won't police themselves. It doesn't matter that you will see them day in and day out and under the most intimate circumstances. A cavity search is NOT a relationship. Give them that inch and they'll make DEMANDS. Next thing you're meeting the mother-in-law for brunch and it's YOUR back up against the wall. Not going to happen.

At the slightest hint of familiarity, erect a barrier. That'll distract them, occupy their energy. You want submission signals. Head down, eyes lowered. Call me sir. Feet off the furniture. Hand off the handle. COMPLIANCE is ideal all true authorities seek.

"But we're just trying not to be alone," Lucy explains.

"I'm sure cozying up to a bunch of assholes really helps with your loneliness." He bristles, a shudder running along his armour. It's a flimsy excuse he's heard a thousand times before. It can only be read as pathetic. Even so, Sophia was angling to get his personal number. Not that he'd answer THE PHONE; sound the sirens! He and the other officials assigned to manage her were the only ones left, her last line of defense, aside from the men.

"What else can dating be in an abandoned asylum," Lucy continued undaunted, "but attempts not to be on your own, to leave your room? It is statistically safe, you're shut in, but also being drained of content, sort of beige. Although you can do art there, there's a space for that, it's got a suicide net. What does that tell you? It's maybe not that satisfying, your nesting egg of strangulated instinct."

"That's what the Yard is for," he spits. "You can go for a run, let your bindings down."

It's true. Snip-snip, they fall into a coil around her ankles to crawl back up later. It is next safest, apart from your room. I mean, it's daylight, you're fenced in, under semi-observation. Except only certain residents will talk to her. There's that element along the wall where it's so easy to slip out . . .

Lucy can hear the carnival from there. The big top is visible above the satiny ribbons of luminous airstrip that billow from the mouth of the atrium.

She tiptoes past the palm-reader in the lobby, now sleeping and always indifferent. The intoxicated party girl with the pointed sparklers waves her in, sets the tone. Lights-out, fantasy fun zone.

She pictures herself a free-wheeling agent, unfettered and in charge. She ignores the persistent slap of an awning, the stifling air, the breaths of mutuality, rare and shallow rales. The flattery of ticker-tape appraisals reiterates her currency. It's wildly fluctuating. It's ultimately undeniable and overwriting. The price of entry, price of staying, price of attention. "Ou est l'égalité, la liberté et de fraternité," elle crie! "Non, il est une economie de commande."

She can feel herself shrinking, monetizing. "So, sweetheart since this was sooo fruitful, how much WAS the price of your drink?" Definitely outside her locus of control. Yes, definitely external but reaching in with each slap . . . "let . . . us . . . see . . . your . . ." A squeeze of her left lung.

And out of the corner of her eye, a floater. The party girl has been replaced is constantly being replaced. A fetishized cheerleader ensemble of virtual part-women spinning around her head. "I'm a P-O-R-N E-F-F-E-C-T."

"IT'S TO FRUSTRATE SOLIDARITY," says the guard, patched-in. "HER NAME IS SOPHIA, BUT YOU CAN CALL HER WHATEVER YOU LIKE."

"No, your face is that revolving general asshole." Lucy tries this old line. He can't hear. It sticks in her mouth. Thick paste of grey krill.

"Deactivating strategies," the guard continues. "Never let them feel secure. At the first sign of propriety, do a sweep of their room, move someone else in, alter the feeding schedule. You want to send a clear message. This is NOT your home. Do NOT get comfortable here. In this crazy-making business, it's either them or you. Remember that."

It was here that Lucy first met Sophia who was already far along some tenuous strip. She's one of those people with the reverse of institutional syndrome who can't tolerate indoors. One moment, she'd be sitting beside you. The next, she'd have shot way out on a band, a smear of filament, to a speck of distant planet.

They were all driven out here in one way or another. For Lucy, a symbolic violence presaged the rest and flipped her into another dimension. Her teeth are on the brick of an outer curtain. A sink trap for her tongue. Perverse surgeries. A PVC tube. Catapult. Finally laid flat. Her face staring down the beady eye of a barrel. Cocked. The gaslight tours that makes you doubt your own subjective reality.

Likewise, Sid, by info wars induced psychosis. A cult-like conditioning that he will be the first to tell you is breaking down. He tends to believe most of the patients are here for that reason, casualties of a failed scientific program.

Who can deny this whole place is pressing toward a fascistic ethos, by aggressive branching ... et partout l'anxiete, l'insecurite, la precarite ... with aspiration and wheezing.

Still, Lucy can yet turn around and safely disappear. They have meds for that, although she can do it all by herself. Attach a spigot and watch the colour drain out. Not so much dead as depressing. Set like a clay foot of paralysis.

But not Sophia who has now run stark into the night and leapt out of her skin in a flayed pirouette. At this point, the guard became pivotal as the last person to have seen her. Officially. That is, until she reappeared in a series of figurations to Lucy. What happened in between is the mystery.

***

WHITE PONIES DON'T EXIST/ MEETS THE SNIVELING CUCK PRINCESS

"My straightjacket's custom made though."
– Jessie Reyez, *Shutter Island*.

"I mean sure, it's called 'Abundant Dick', but if you think you get to choose your associates then you're on the other side. And guess who that is in a borderline facility? That's right, other patients. Mostly, this new dangerous breed who congregates along the fourth wall and at off-grid parties, because AFFINITY. It's all about who can hang. In unredeemable damnation.

You think I don't try to hitch a white pony out of here? You think I'm not trying right now? 'Hey, you there with your dignified, visiting curator of the new iconography who likes weirdos, could I perhaps catch a lift?'

And do you know what he's probably thinking? Neither do I because SILENCE. Just kidding. He's thinking 'WHITE PONIES DON'T EXIST.' They are just closet unicorns with Tetsuo horns. Four times in one night is a bit iron man. Conclusion. Ponies are sex addicts. Don't say 'not all ponies'. And in any case, he's not going to redeem you either. Speed your own trip! With inventions by the hard-working men of science.

God does hate a coward. He must. Next rung, right-side leg paresthesia. I volunteered for the botched medical experiments. Again. Seventy-odd chemical jolts to burn the spiders from my veins. And you thought I was un-pristine before. Yes of course they're saying I did it to myself. That's how it is here."

'WELL NOTHING BAD EVER HAPPENED TO ME,' says the goodie nurse who gave me rough oral intubation of charcoal sludge when I first arrived. 'BECAUSE I DON'T PUT MYSELF IN THOSE SITUATIONS. AND I ALWAYS WEAR A UNIFORM.'

"Okay. Except did you ever notice how he likes to sort us into faeries and trolls rolling around in the muck in what is some sort of leotard? Or how he doesn't really mind the brazen ones when he's inviting them back to his room to thread your insecurities for you, or manipulate what you like and don't like in music? I mean lesbihonest, are inflated slavering mouths really your taste? Yeah, they are now, but . . . And does your whole order really prefer short hair? Or are you perhaps a bit self-mutilating too?

But I sympathize. There was a time I was arrogant too. Not a goodie nurse but . . . something. Oh right, aversive. Yes, I know I'm still pretty off-putting. Apparently, spitting is not a very ideal feminine. According to the bourgeois curator pony.

'I see, and would you prefer I spit in your mouth instead? Well, don't say I never asked.'

"I can't help but notice that, although excessively exercising, the pony, for some reason, avoids the yard. No, nothing to do with significant other wives behind forbidden doors. Nothing related to how he's not around on weekends, or how his profile is hidden, or how he erupts into swearing in his bathroom if you drop by his perfectly contrived show room unannounced. Twice. No, nothing to do with that. He's just not that into sunlight. It happens. When you're a sensitive mythical animal."

'I THINK THAT WOULD BE A GOOD GAME FOR US PRINCESS. PRETENDING,' he says while pointing his non-symbolic drill at me and wanting to make me one of the pieces in his revolving collection. Tuesday. 'STILL YOU'RE VERY DANGEROUS TO ME AND MY LIFE. SO, DON'T GO STICKING YOUR NOSE WHERE IT DOESN'T BELONG.'

He therefore prefers to give carousel rides at night with all the curtains drawn and Liz Phair dimly whirring. As in, your face reminds me of a flower. Kind of like it's underwater. An exhibit wrapped in plastic. I'm an old school romantic.

Except I don't like imperiled realities with homicidal overtones. And why would anyone play with me? I wouldn't. I say the same thing I say to all my suitors and their weapons of choice. 'You can either use that thing or put it down.'"

'YOU'RE VERY TOUGH FOR A SNIVELING PRINCESS.'

As if I had a choice. But that's right. And so as soon as you're asleep I'll steal your key to the room with your nonexistent wives and tell them everything they wanted to know about you but were afraid to ask and set them free.

'IT'S AMAZING NONE OF US HAS KILLED YOU YET SUGARPLUM TROLL.'

Yes, well better luck next time. And also, with your rotating pressed flower exhibit."

***

THE HANDLER IS A WOLFSANGEL/ BUT WITH GOOD MUSICAL TASTES

"It is a well-defined form of anxiety. You feel the enemy is within; its characteristic ardor compels you, with inflexible urgency, to do what you do not want to do; you feel the end, the transient, before which you vainly attempt to flee to an uncertain future."
– Sabina Spielrein, *Destruction as Cause of Becoming*

"Next Level Dating. I sold my gateway panties to Icke the Dirty Old Toad and followed Sophia down the Funnel of Love Squrl cover. I think everyone knows its basic shape is tapering circles of ledges that grow smaller as they descend so as to get more constricting.

There are twelve wards in the severe division with an obelisk rudely prodding you along; beyond that is the ocean. And we're only at, well, whatever number is plagues. That is one of the hazards when you're lowering yourself along its segmented thread on a deep tunnel expedition and there are no reliable authorities. It's actually a health crisis, plagues is, and deserves a class action to be perfectly honest. Well, against whoever the god of this place is, or one of his local representatives.

I guess the pressing existential question is what is it about the fears and anxieties of our times, and others' internal realities,

SUSPECT M

and whatever other fillers I'm absorbing, that makes all these suitors want to choke and gag and sever me? And who is my most spiritual enemy? As in who most wants me dead?

That does seem to be the primary goal of this latest app of the love cure. Merging with various suitors arrayed in a deli platter around your head that wants to give you forced paroxysms and dysmorphic grind-core. As in, I'm not happy until it's basically torture. How many times have we all heard that before, amiright? And ego integration. And getting to know your professional savior.

Of course, there's always the gratuitous first date where you meet me for coffee in the lobby and think, 'What is this person doing here? There must be some kind of clerical error.' Well, you can thank the asylum for that, with its generous admittance policy. But also, what did you expect? Frothing? I assure you frothing is a very rare symptom and mostly kept under wraps with anticonvulsants and dimmed lights. Mostly. And otherwise, vastly dissimilar animals corralled in a fictional Chinese dictionary entry of Trans-Allegheny.

Such as, ever heard of the inhabitants of Shutter Island whose straightjackets are custom made? Sixteenth century dancing plagues that spread as contagion throughout the French countryside unto death and ravaged feet? Ever heard of repressive parts of contemporary Turkey where women suffer blind conversions? Ever heard of needles and clamps and hot wax that failed to disprove anesthesia? Of countless men washed up after wars in fits and terrors and phantom limbs? Ever heard of other men? The neurasthenics of the new industrial society with diseases of the spleen and no womb? That is so all about me and my documentary of lying. How do you know what I do in my private time? Think about it Seth. It's the girl you don't want to get stuck talking to at a party, but then have to apologize to later for doubting her genuineness.

I am that self-obsessed and spiritual. Never mind the mystery of the missing Sophia P. Never mind the black beast of medicine. I'm the above ground star because my doctor said so. I'm the most parasitic and plastic. One of those emotional vampire trilogies you've probably never heard of unless you are: a. in the medical establishment that is never currently taking referrals; b. visiting men-only sites with 12-step escape plans; or, c. watching misogynistic psycho-thrillers.

While I mention it, please forget about nymphomaniac fatal attraction monsters now collapsed under DSM version whatever warning labels. Those are just propaganda flicks manufactured by deep underground military bases. That's DUMBS for the uninitiated. I suppose I have been spending a lot of time with Sid and paranoia, and these colliding worlds become more integrated. Just because you're suggestible doesn't mean they're not trying to extract your life force and trap your soul.

Just ask Icke who's now live-streaming footage of the trauma-based experiments from the lip of the funnel. However unsavory and responsible for those frog tie embellishments on the arc en ciel, he does seem to have hit upon the only reliable etiology for certain strains of resistant personality.

Yes, I'm referring to the experiments that got CIA university funding and were later implicated in the sixties scoop, now reformed into a supposedly public system of surrogate parenting. If you have no way to expel those incursions into your actual person, well, don't be surprised if that leads to certain maladaptive mutations. I mean, it's just a bit coincidental how many of us who were in those are now stricken with acronyms with a lot of D's is all I'm saying.

Also, isn't failure of empathy a funny thing to say to someone with absorbency and contagion? Would you say that about the Convulsionaries of Saint Medard, hmm? I bet you would, too. And then it would be the saints you'd grandfather into your secular museum of pathology, like the great and powerful Charcot.

What you MEAN to say is: empathizes with the wrong things, and too much. Such as do you know what Sophia finds triggering? Family. Community. Concentric circles of exclusionary. So, if you could, please adjust your art curriculum for that and warnings. Just so she doesn't stick a knife into her hand again.

And we can hold more than one introjected objects in our head at once and not split black. More than most people, even. Such as, The Handler is a Wolfsangel is the most banal type of suitor who collects women as tinder but has unusual musical acumen. He also hosts parties. They're just on a semi-autonomous retreat the size of a small village. See?

Okay, maybe banal is the wrong word. A rival authority who, nonetheless, exists in some accord with the institutional reality. It must. Because everybody knows; even off-duty guards go there. It's an open secret, in other words. He's sending out engraved invitations on little bleached skulls, like chiming snow globes, to his mixed social where a steady blue light burns. Who doesn't like to snuggle up next to some warm ember? Nobody, that's who.

Still it's important to really read someone's ABOUT ME section before meeting them in person. For example:

'I'M ON THE STEPPE HUNTING FALCONS AMONGST NECKBEARDS . . . INFILTRATE THE RURAL WHITE

TRASH AND BLEND IN AMONGST THE LOCALS
... CUT OFF SUPPLIES ... STARVE THE URBANITES ...
PEOPLE WARFARE WILL WORK . . I'M A BIT NERVOUS
AND SOMETIMES ACCIDENTALLY MISSPEAK OR BLOW
THINGS UP.'

Don't worry, it's only trying to goad local authorities to arrest him. They are, so far, refusing because not enough beds at the inn even though Sucidesque and wants to take the village with him.

I thought I was a performance artist. He's Trevor Something Does-Not-Exist and welcome to my nightmare, with rotting teeth that are driving me insane and a cocaine drip for the pain. Someone's got to pay for that because we all have to contribute to the facility's financial viability. So, get your neo-Strasserite youth out there boy, with homophobic results. But don't bare those teef, Wolfsangel. Because HORROR.

That's right. Another 'I tried–being a homeless and gay' self-hating cliché. Another backstory. But now doing very well for himself thank you, and BTW, he's the one who kills the lead actress in the remake. Not the flakey Richard Gere clown from the lobby, but the Tom Berenger combat trauma victim. Substitute wretched teeth for pock marks and a hellhole in Lashkargah for Vietnam.

Note to self, use a megaphone. DO NOT DATE THE HANDLER. He is clearly a mouthpiece for the Great Animator of this world. Also, a psychopath. That's what he said. Except they don't call it that anymore, so get ye to the borderline facility. Or a base camp somewhere in its vicinity.

'Don't feel too badly about your serial dating,' he assures me. 'You know Emma Goldman? She did a lot of people, but she just talked about other things.' Good advice, Strasserite fellow whore.

SUSPECT M

I'm serious about that. Thank you for not being another penal guard. Yes, I do reserve my utmost for him. I guess it's because I first believed his duty was to protect me. Just symbolically, because I told him everything that was happening. I reported it. And guess what? 'Not my jurisdiction and can't do nuttin' for you ma'am.'

Point taken. Emma Goldman wasn't just another Russian slut. She apparently talked about OTHER THINGS when not prancing around like a numbskull stripper. Like what else is there? And are you perhaps unaware that she was, well, Goldman? Isn't that taking your cooptation of leftist icons a bit far? I mean just for a third positionist? I know. Not a real Nazi serial killer. What happens to the tinder after you collect it in a pile and light a fire under it is really not your responsibility.

'WE DON'T WANT SUPREMACY. WE WANT OUT. IF SURVEILLANCE IS EVERYWHERE IN MODERN SOCIETY, AND MODERN SOCIETY IS 80% URBAN. THEN MY DUDE, GO BACK TO THE COUNTRY. SONS OF ODIN T-SHIRT. THAT'S WHERE I'M A VIKING.'

He spends all day painting his walls with the Psychic Rites of a Killer, then comes and asks how I'm doing. He's nice to me in other words. That's what they're like. Not all of them but. You know who wasn't nice? The underground film star with his ice pick heart who wouldn't let me visit unless strip searched first and taking a baton for the team with the camera rolling. No doubt it will later appear in some pirated stills of the new iconography. And all because he's emotionally scared of me. So now you're in my litany, fancy word for grievance, fancy word for complaining. Also, you think you're scared of me now? Hold on.

I'm about to give another orthodox performance to earn my keep in the facility. But am I really? Orthodox and any trouble for anyone if so easily choreographed and blocked?

Did I invite him in, you ask? This enemy which everyone agrees upon is in there, but then doesn't want to talk about what he's DOING. (Well I do. He's building a living museum of pathology!) Do you mean is he like a vampire who cares about consent? Maybe. We'll ask him if we're ever caught in the lair. We'll ask Sophia in the sub-basements, if she's still down there and not merely trapped in a film, vibrating. 'So Sophia, did he get your consent before he made that eternal Purgative Cure gif and distributed it to everyone? Are you, perhaps, performing your eroto-mania at the behest of the dead-eyed camera jockey who never takes off his onesie? Have they given you any satisfaction survey about how you like your new JOB?'"

***

THE ONE GOOD DICK ROMEO/A FALSE MEMORY IMPLANT

"And if I go while you're still here . . . know that I live on . . . vibrating to a different measure . . . behind a thin veil you cannot . . . see through. You will not see me . . . so you must have faith."
– Emily Dickinson, "Faith"

"Someone had to go in and plant the false memory to prevent I'm Miss World's absorption of others' worse realities, victims and abusers alike, by a parasite who wants to infect everyone with her erotic, dancing plague unto death. That was the assignment. It was a method we could easily access, having taken to it naturally during our early DID training at the academy. A matter of embedding in your surroundings, while at the same time observing even yourself as if from a distance and taking good field notes such as an ethnographer criminologist named Romeo might.

The setting was Pick Ur Own Retreat. That's the alternative where the former Wolfsangels escaped and were building a separatist colony in thrall to a new moon. Even though fully documented elsewhere, it seemed important to really look at what went on at their ceremonies, whose purpose was not so much to atone as to relinquish any guilt that might have attached itself to their mortal acts. To burn it off, ritually. See Alex Jones tape.

It was for this reason that the cremation had been concealed in a grove where history had stopped. At the end of the line, slingshot to atom bomb, the arrested heart of the forest where bad things cycle inevitably, and all the victims stay the same. With replacements. You can have a virtual harem of Sophias, says their promo video. You can call them whatever you like. You can call them Little Red, or Justine. Virtue, it said on the cover.

That's always the original crime scene, as investigated by the one good dick, Romeo, who once took on the entire penal force that had blocked his attempts to put out public warnings about true fairytale patterns. As in versus. Which, no doubt, some will find to be a violation of the integrity of the institution. Much as they did, the fact was, he was a lesbian. We're going to do it anyway. This reflexive journaling on the prior day to day of certain subjects. As the least fiction we can fathom at the moment.

Was he there? Not exactly. He was still one foot in the Broadway nights. Which is close enough to say that, should anyone debate you on the existence of profiling, please refer them to Romeo's geographic theory. It did have some traction amongst those preoccupied with pre-empting serial transgressions, i.e., the CIA. Hunter. Poacher. Troller. Trapper. That was maybe his best-known taxonomy. Just spare us your 'we don't do profiling here' objections, penal force. You're textbook.

Apart from being an expert, Romeo tried to alert the facility and the broader society to unusual activities concentrated around the retreat and related to dating. A rash of missing persons was not accounted for by the usual attrition or transience, but by some

SUSPECT M

more sinister element. He had further traced these to a triangle joining the retreat to the neglected garden and the Broadway nights of the DTES, with these latter two seeming entry points to the forest's funnel-like vortex. Some called it the surrogate parenting to trafficking pipeline.

It was in the eye of this triangle that Romeo first met Sophia during one of the SRO conversions where he was appointed to spearhead a special unit. This lesbian in an old boy's playpen. Despite any resemblances between him and the victims. Resemblances that could sometimes be uncanny amongst many of those drawn to, but not entirely living in, the DTES. Who were not held as if by some centrifugal pull with no escape but could mostly come and go as they liked. No, not tourists, but also not to be confused with those who prided themselves on the professional thickness of their lizard-skin which sometimes hardened into malice. Who disguised their ignorance with bravado? And so, it was not surprising that Sophia should mistake Romeo for a friend.

He wasn't without armour. That's what criminologist guards do. They wear uniforms. They shave their heads and bleach their skulls in sympathetic agony. They carve deVries into their forearms and wear steel-toed boots and blast NIN into headphones while hiking up and down a mountain highway tracked with tears. Not hitchhiking, thank you. How else can you pull off Reservoir Dogs and Paul Bernardo in the same seminar? But please don't think that makes him victim and conflation. He is not being a cuck princess right now. This is tough guy act and a no-feelings liar. This is Romeo.

I don't blame anyone for thinking us incapable of something more than just another romantic murder-suicide. We are, after all and for the most part, the substance equivalent of strippers with a politics of dirty protest. We are after all wandering from pillar to post and don't nobody want to love a ghost who's turning invisible now. Except the ones that do. Her family. Her community of washer women. That's the banned version we most want to see happen. I mean, after we go inside the false grandmother and the reversal inception, we light a fire under him. Under all of them. These transgressives."

***

THE ALIEN DOCTORS/A PROBE SENT INTO THE TUNNELS

"It's become clear to me now that we've been abducted by the alien doctors. I'm not kidding; that's what they were called. The specialists who threatened the respectability of their profession by associating with her. The black beast of medicine who regarded her as something between a caged animal and an opponent in a chess game. This fact is now buried under classified, specious endnotes. Still their heads keep poking up.

I know you want to believe it's the lone gunman theory. The blue-eyed star of all their videos who never takes off his onesie. Or the gang of pagan neckbeards prancing in the forest whose claims against the establishment are totally unfounded. But, the fact is, these transgressives wouldn't get anywhere without cover of the facility. Without the chanting townsfolk who chased her out in the first place but now want to pursue her paranormally. What's the word for that again? Oh yeah, NIMBY tourist.

Channeling these earlier inhabitants, Crepitus suggested I might expel the contents of my bad self. My so-called daylight hallucinations, for purposes of catharsis. The hypnosis test. It's the second-to-last one. Can she make revelatory the contents of her terrifying visions? How suggestable is she? Here goes trances! Apply steady pressure to forehead and report faithfully the pictures, ideas, and emojis that pass before your inner eye."

***

"Welcome to my nightmare. Or his. I will remember you.

I accepted one of the bleached-skull invitations to his mixed social in the forest. The Handler, who is connected, and Sid's associate, though he rarely goes there, had originally confiscated these, along with some razor blades and Clorox, but then had inexplicably given them back. I guess so he could keep bleaching away evidence. Whose skulls? Small animals, of course. What, did you think they were human? No, the side rooms are for animal rendering. Never mind the footage where you can hear a distinctly human voice screaming. That's just info wars and doctoring. No one was ever burned alive here on a pyre of tinder.

If you're expecting just one Wolfsangel, you're in the wrong place. These hunt and trap and poach and troll in packs. That's the point of it. They're a band of brother-outsiders. A fortress and a swarm. Some of them are more committed to infiltrating the channels of power, while others are in it for lulz and cracking heads. The Handler tries to accommodate both."

"This is where we all link up," he says, "to the new members.

Leave it to Billy the Roper to spread puerile acrimony. There are only two ways of tracing your identity in traditional belief. There's the vein of Varg, who as a pan-Odalist, projects Norse paganism to all descendants. They're federalists who want an imperium and think blood quantum trumps regional specificity. Whereas we favour a decentralization bordering on wildness. A nativism. But operating in the narrow window of western colonial settler, with cowboy pirate ideation. It's more cultural, to be honest."

"The Handler himself is of mixed origin. On the one side, his cousin was a prospector for the Wolfsangels. On the other, his dad was a guard. And you know what they say about the blue code. They have each other's backs. What is maybe less known is that the two sides are often in cahoots. So, a lot of the penal guards are connected too. Why do you think they have so many have start-ups on retirement? In fact, there was a time when just belonging to the force made you an honorary member. These days, they have to conduct recruitment drives and all under the radar.

They've seated the baby-faced one whose profile says a few extra pounds at the entrance to screen guests.

'What's the broom-handle shiv for?'

'Domestic role-play.'

'Are you supposed to be girls?'

'Someone must think so.'

'Well, show us your price of entry.'

'Alright then.'

'And what's with the red cap?'

'It's so the hunter doesn't shoot me as I deliver a package to my false grandmother. It's very remote out here you know.'

And with that, I am on his insides now."

* * *

THE MYSTERY OF THE MISSING SOPHIA P./DELIVERS A PACKAGE TO HER FALSE GRANDMOTHER

"Where, oh, where have you been my love?
Where, oh, where can you be?
It's been so long, since the moon has gone.
and oh what a wreck you've made me

Are you there, over the ocean?
Are you there, up in the sky?
Until the return of my love
This lullaby

My Hope is on the horizon
Every face, it's your eyes I can see
I plead, I pray through each night and day
Our embrace is only a dream.

And as sure as days come from moments
Each hour becomes a life's time
When she'd left, I'd only begun this lullaby"
– Queens of the Stone Age, "This Lullaby"

SUSPECT M

You think this is repetition? Let me tell you a story and let me tell you a story and. You're right. That's how they establish the one law. Do you remember what it is? That's why we have to repeat everything, going over and over again the same fixation of why, at some points, was there only one set of footprints? Because that's when he carried her . . . then cut in the chirping choir of insect worrying . . ." ohhhhh, we should've put a tracking device on her . . . we should've trimmed back the overgrown wiry snatches . . . we should've not with the spikes . . . we should've not with the sledgehammer to the carts . . . we should've not with the upturned river camp . . . and pinch it off."

Okay. Now regress way back to what I said in one of my early profiles, that if you were a fan of the inmate rebellion, as is perhaps most conspicuous in the works of Tarantino, then skip to the end. In the kitchen with a broom handle. It's a shiv. A splinter into the closing dark of an eye. Zedd's dead. No, he is risen.

There are several theories about the whereabouts of Sophia P., whose dating handle was 'Little Red.' This refers to her first brush with the asylum at 12, in which she woke from what was to be a routine visit to find a cauterizing iron had been taken to her small, red flame for the crime of self-emanating. "Excessively," said her foster mother and the medical establishment.

You don't believe they did this? It was common practice and there's an article about it in Fake News, if that's not reliable enough for you.

'Didn't work,' Sophia liked to say many years later. The wilful girl equivalent of that libertine who wrote on his cell walls in feces. The wilful girl equivalent of folklore.

She strutted the ribbons of Broadway night and cavorted with the other residents, her boyfriend who looked out for her like family, and who she did favours for in return, such as delivering packages to his associate who hosted parties.

You might be surprised who went there. Or not. His band of organized neckbeards, of course. They had their own clubhouse across a service road where they held regular meetings about such matters as how to defend themselves from the new barbarian hordes on one front and Billy's purity purges on another, and on how to improve their image. Also, a lot of off-duty guards. Some businessmen, one of them on town council. Local lounge acts. And lots and lots of 'girls', as they called them.

But the boyfriend kept his distance."

'They're watching me,' he told Sophia. 'They're building a case to make me their patsy.'

And 'they' is never a good sign. He was, in fact, watching them watch him with a set of tiny binoculars out his window. They were sometimes so blatant as to park outside his house. They also had eyes everywhere, as he was fond of saying. They infiltrate your social media with thots. The unmarked car was mostly for intimidation.

And so, he devised methods to skirt detection, using Sophia as go-between, carrying packages wrapped in floral cellophane. An indispensable link in a smooth-running chain. That is until.

On this occasion, instead of taking the package and leaving her to mingle with his guests, The Handler shunted her off to his trailer.

She had never been there before; it seemed a breach of etiquette to be alone with him. She reassured herself that her boyfriend must know, what with the two of them being so close.

Nervous, she scanned the room. It had pile upon pile of salvaged odds and ends. Despite doing well for himself, The

SUSPECT M

Handler cultivated the impression of a survivalist farmer. His face and neck were nearly covered in a mass of wire wool. His ruddy knuckles were stained with dirt. He displayed his signature wretched teeth, which he refused to have fixed. The simple style of his ancestors was good enough for him–and should be for everyone. His appearance was his main rift with rivals who wished to project clean-cut success.

Amidst the many layers, Sophia noticed in one corner a collection of purses, women's jewelry, and what looked like ID.

'Who do those belong to?' she blurted.

'Some working girls,' was his swift answer. He was now clearly on edge.

Wanting to sooth the tension Sophia remembered amongst the gifts a pot of butter, his favourite cooking medium, and so dug it out and placed it on the table before him.

He instantly perked up, and hungrily ran his tongue along his protruding upper lip.

'Would you be so sweet, dear, as to remove the lid?'

'Of course,' she said, and had barely peeled it off when he shoved his muzzle in and began feverishly lapping, growling and gnashing.

He didn't let up until he had swallowed the whole thing. Then, leaning back, hands resting on his curved belly, he casually sucked grease from the gristle around his mouth and looked her over.

It is at this point that she sometimes gets away, when he's temporarily sated. You know that excuse of needing to go to the bathroom to sneak out of a bad date? Well, the girl with the red hood invented that.

It wasn't without a fight. He tried to chain her to a bed by the wrist as she was leaving the bathroom. Luckily, she had earlier noticed a large knife on his counter and hid it in her skirts."

'All the better to slice you open like a swollen grape,' she thought, and plunged it into his gut.

She did finally weaken him enough to escape, though it was with a concussion and dislocated shoulder that she stumbled back through the shroud of forest and found the nearby highway where a couple picked her up. After she dropped the knife, of course.

And she did report the incident. She did. That's one of things that came out in Romeo's unpublished memoirs. But the crown determined she wasn't a credible witness with her clothes still drenched in blood and a cuff dangling off her. The key was found in the Handler's pants pocket. He was being treated in an adjoining room of the same hospital.

Apart from losing three litres of blood, he had a punctured lung; and his hands were in tatters. 'Defensive wounds,' wrote the guard who put his clothes into evidence, though they weren't tested until seven years later. Had they done this at the time, they would have found traces of two other partygoers who were missing. Had they visited his lair, they would have found their identification and purses. Had they searched the extended grounds, they would have found his cremation of care.

Curiously, it's the versions where she escapes by her own wit and courage, and sometimes taking an older female with her, that were most banned. Even once the truth about his retreat was public, there remained problems of jurisdiction. And so, Sophia's case was never admitted into evidence and she wasn't allowed to testify.

That's not all that was repressed.

SUSPECT M

'He didn't act alone,' said one witness, but then quickly added it was just her opinion. And she didn't know anything after his associates paid her a visit. There was also said to be a misplaced tape where a penal guard engaged in a violent group ritual at the retreat. A certain John de Sade, whose appetite for gruesome fairy tales was well-known on the street, as was his practice of driving his victims off-grid where whatever happens is someone else's business.

And who do you report that to, by the way? Nobody. He's THE LAW. Although you can tell everyone you know and create a wiki entry. Which is what they did.

Sophia wasn't always so lucky. For the most part, it's the same victims as ever. They say they're post-this and neo-that. Still, there's a revival of past doctrines and lesser-known figures and iconic imagery. The only slightly altered backward Zed on their backs in bright red feathers. Their nostalgia for the unpolluted streams of pre-urban man. The revisionist history of their grandparents. Do you want to interfere with their traditions that go back centuries? Well, that's because you're a Feminazi. Long live total liberty."

***

"Having subdued me in the forest, they transported me by convoy to the deep basements–the very same annals of cell and antechamber where the phantom parasite remains, unhappily repressed.

I had already had a preview and, horrified, dropped the magical key in the blood and fled. I then told everyone about it to keep myself safe. I've found no one is ever very happy with your curious investigations of their innermost phone contacts.

They don't like you entering of their hidden rooms with stolen keys. Be prepared for that. They turn on you. Don't be surprised if it's military. A lot of former abductees report that. DUMBS. That's where they keep all his former lovers, forever wedded to his tilting vessel.

To get there, you need to traverse 'No Pussy Pass'. It's in 1915 black and white. You are compelled to leave your body behind and follow the man in the rabbit costume through a wild field into a hollow where you will slip and slide downward to land on a heap of sticks and dry leaves. So, that's where it is. The secret entrance to the funnel. The back door, as it were.

I can see now why Sid didn't want to breach them. They've set up a pre-taped interview at the crossing where, to be let in, you have to convince them that you can suffer the same consequences as men. You have to sell yourself and prove that it's all consensual. Way past consensual. That you are responsible for yourself and everything that happens to you. Also, for the spreading modern degeneracy. That you really are 'I'm Miss World' absorbent. A Serbian masochist who has signed an oral contract."

***

THE ONE GOOD DICK ROMEO/ BLUE EYE HAS LEFT HIS CHAMBER

"Hi. It's Romeo again. Copy that. It seems there's more to say on the Blue Eye profile. I think we nailed the wrong guy. It's possible the Beta uprising was a false flag to flush out suggestables. Apparently, Sebastian really is a saint. Seems it's that another Greek letter, Alpha. That's how he describes himself. Sexy Beast.

I've obtained a recording of his recent chat with Lucy, where he references a past date who wanted to be knocked out and stuffed into a trunk as a form of roleplay. No doubt there's a whole side conversation to be had about former abuse victims participating in hard core fantasies. Stick a pin in it.

He then asks if she's ever seen "The Vanishing" and admits his obsession with the unsolved case of the murdered night nurse from 1962. He's invited Lucy to pose in a series of photos. In black and white. In the first, she would be standing naked in front of her window, the one overlooking the yard and facing the rooms on the other side. In the meantime, he's rendered a series of six sketches, which Lucy has taped to her wall. No, we can't locate the former date to confirm. In fact, he made no mention of her name in keeping with serial dater etiquette.

I bet you're thinking what I am. It's the same MO. Death Drive. And there's something eerie about them casually discussing abduction, with him dismissing all of her precautions as after-the-fact.

A couple more things. As I said, the recording is recent. That means Lucy's still active on his profile. There's something about him she finds compelling. Or maybe it's the severe ward itself. She's been inviting other patients up to her room, maybe thinking it's safer, a locus of control. Of course, we know better.

Next, our perp, Blue Eye. He's confined to the basements at the extreme opposite end of the facility. His excursions during daylight hours are restricted. He's still got a music shop down there and has started making electric guitars. My sense is that's a cover for his starring role in the asylum's trauma re-enactments. There is one they call "The Drowning Chamber". Seems it was the final test of hysteria in more barbaric times. Does she have an unconscious, so she can swim, or will she drown? I've attached an addendum of Jung talking to Joyce about his Schizophrenic daughter. Crepitus definitely gives it his own twist. I'll have more on that later, but suffice it to say, I'm not sure he's on our side. He's under a lot of pressure to keep the asylum viable and is taking kick-backs from the drug companies. His coupling of the love cure and paranormal tours in itself is dubious. Run any communications with him by me first.

Back to Blue Eye. He's a rough prospect at this point. Don't think they'd have much luck billing him as romantic lead. Mickey Rourke meets "Fifty Shades". His blue eye is so receded it's an open socket in a moonscape of grey pork chop. Death warmed over, as they say. You can't just keep people in underground tunnels like mole rats.

SUSPECT M

I'm sure you follow but, given that the whole middle has dropped out for both patients, it implies a direct passageway between the Abundant Dick dating app, Lucy's laptop, and the deep basements. My gut tells me it's many corridors. How many I don't know; it could be infinite, a massive system of tree roots reaching in a downward direction, with connecting nodes. If you take Lucy's chats alone, there's the long-haul truck driver. There's the occultist who ranted about his ex being a bi-sexual slut. There's the baby-faced former club member.

Something stuck with me about that last one–his assertion that the level of corruption amongst penal guards was no greater than that of Wolfsangels. I'm starting to think it's related to inaction on this file. They've erected a wall of excuses to block my efforts. Problems of jurisdiction. Of violating the patient's Miranda rights. Yeah, the patient they keep in a dungeon. Lack of resources, given the push on speeding tickets. Let's just hope he likes to drive fast."

* * *

SID THE PATSY/FRESH GOAT WITH HIS THROAT CUT

There comes a point in every spiritual journey when you realize that trust is a major issue in relationships and most of your suitors are armed paranoiacs given to rival factions and easily incited to turn on each other. That there's a code. Yes, it might be blue. And loose lips do sink ships, despite that being an odd thing for a bourgeois, curator pony to say.

"The next time he invites you to the retreat, accept," Sid had said. "We need to find out what they're burning and if that Alex Jones tape is real.

Also, he'll expect you to have a package, as a gift."

"Is that what Sophia was doing for you, delivering packages?"

"Possibly, for convenience, and to do me a favour. What are you implying?"

"Nothing. But why would you conspire against him when he's your friend? Are you thinking of taking over his operation?"

"I'm not conspiring against him. I just don't need to tell him everything. I'm not his slave."

"Are you sure you're not his slave? He seems to control you. I've seen how he bombards you with ultra-violent memes paired with certain phrases. And while he's very wealthy, you take all the risk and live in a small room."

SUSPECT M

"You can't go around saying things like that."

"Oh, but I thought the two of you shared everything."

"What do you mean everything?"

"Well such as Sophia. It seems obvious that he was involved with her, and that you also felt some affection. Or was it something more sinister?"

"You really know how to break a man down. I feel like it's been you all along."

"Yes, it's the building back up that's harder. But don't you think it's time for you to stand up and be the suitor now, and to wear the goat skin?"

***

PRONOIA OF SOPHIA P.

The first breaks in the breakaway tunnels began as a tapping on thin-skin membrane, a tracing of naval under water drum vibrating. Began as I remember how we got here and how it all began, the Ecstasy of Hedy Lamarr school-girls snuggling fingers darting in. I remember the slip of a tap opening a small red flame sister cells dividing. I remember in rippling blades of (was it blood or water?) engorging. I remember, broken and convulsing, a spire shot up, the cap off a cascade of sparks igniting.. I remember make of thy sacred enemy a totem and incinerate him. I remember all the times you escaped humming, "Don't worry." And I love you, forever and always, Amen.

ROMEO 3/CREPITUS IS A FAKE

"It's me again. Your favorite dick, Romeo. Quick memo on Lucy's falling out with Crepitus. It seems he had confided to her that he thought all women were crazy bitches and only wanted to counsel men. That's right, the manosphere is in the asylum! Crepitus is a red-pilled member of the MRA and has adopted Jordan Peterson as an influence. He's become a quack, in other words.

He hasn't scheduled any appointments with Lucy since, and has issued a gag order, citing doctor-patient privilege. He still needs to project compassion in case he wants to stick his almost imperceptibly tiny needle into someone.

This setback with her analyst, a parental figure, was definitely a factor in Lucy's relapse with the Blue Eye profile. She has started referring to Crepitus as "not a real doctor" and "wears a rug". These revelations appear not to have been catastrophic. Rather, her attitude is more one of being accustomed. I think that is more dangerous, frankly–that she might view Crepitus and Blue Eye as equivalent harms, and even prefer the pure Alpha.

In any case, we already have one missing patient and can't risk losing another. So, here's what we're going to do. Extreme measures. We issue a global dictum. No more penetrations of the facility, from any access point. No one gets in or out. Get one of the girls to draw it up. You know what the reformed

French-Israeli said about "love with no hands" It's just any hole, not picky? Well, the opposite of that. Seal off all the holes. We need to send a clear message that we're not a receptacle for every malignant stray the good town folk can't handle. We care about what we let in. No live or dead meat.

Also, I'd contacted the rural detachment who took away their guns and upped their meds. Still a couple of the abduction fetishists are transmitting scenarios and planning to relocate next door. Here's what I think. We set up decoys at the leak sites, using the dating app as a basecamp. Several smut-mouthed online dolls. And a supportive wifey. Sporty spice, gardening gnome, naughty nun. Depending on the perp's tastes. When the mission's over, tell the girls they can use the fake profiles to vet their former fiancés."

***

BONFIRE OF THE WOLFSANGELS/ THE INCEPTION OF CARE

There aren't only the three alternatives. There's the banned version where Little Red escapes by virtue of her own wit and courage. Taking an older woman with her, the two of them wait under shroud of trees for the next lighting of the cremation. Sometimes, he gets boiled in a pot. So that's more boiling than cremating. But that's when there's only one of them. At some point, they are joined by a monkey who brings the spark. Monkey is the right monkey for the job when the time comes and doesn't care about such things as being nice and not hurting our enemies who deserve it.

Also, you know when the baby-faced Wolfsangel asked to see my price of entry? He was referring to my package which I had wheeled in on a serving cart. "I'm one of the Marys," I said, "but the petting zoo only had goats."

"Well it better be live at least because the Handler likes to make the first cut himself and he wants it fresh."

Sid bleated.

There's something else he said in his exit interview. Yes, we let him go to become one of the famous forest kinder in exchange for some information.

His brother, John de Sade, was the original guard who once drove our patient to the town's edge where he pushed her out of his vehicle with nothing to cover herself but snow.

ALEKSANDRA McHUGH

It was in the wee hours that de Sade was savaged with a drill, a golf club and rock-in-a-sock by thugs after a monkey falsely claimed he was a podiatrist. That's right, podiatrist. Anyway. It was after smashing his face the pair took him from a doorway back to his second home in the country so that his wife and kids wouldn't have to witness the grisly scene, it being no fault of theirs.

He could not remember what happened but woke several hours later with injuries to 28 different parts of his body and having been peed on as a tree, which, though it is a humiliation move really and doesn't hurt much. Not to mention he'd been hit so hard with one of his golf clubs it snapped, his legs punctured with a drill, and a spirit level was used to fracture his skull, cheek and eye socket.

Finally, he was left with bleeding on the brain, a collapsed lung, a broken hand, multiple cuts and bruises, and marks to his neck suggesting the use of an electric cable. His assailants then dragged him unconscious and bloody into his wine cellar, where he was finally abandoned.

He was nonetheless saved by some grace to live out his many final days in a privatized P3 hospice/organ harvesting facility attached to a very expensive feeding tube that drained his estate of funds.

Police are also searching for three shadowy figures who beat a man, Tommy Icke, in several separate instances in the city's fashion district where he gave advanced sewing lessons.

In one clip found on security cameras, the figures are seen to congregate on a staircase outside the ground floor shoe boutique and smoke a cigarette. The other clip is vicious, as it should be. In it, one suspect in a hooded red sweatshirt delivers several swift kicks to Icke's bulging torso.

SUSPECT M

A short time later, the three returned to pummel him in a sleeping bag that he had meant for one of his models to wear as an exoskeleton.

He was not discovered until the following morning around 7 a.m., where he didn't immediately die, but suffered from his wounds, undergoing hours of prolonged agony. All of it was caught on tape. It's what he would have wanted, really.

Zombie's moment of terror rather came after he passed out in the parking lot in back of a bakery, which he really should not have done. He awoke to the sound of taunts as he was being punched and kicked by three enthusiastic assailants. He was then reported to have said "they press ganged me" but failed to report the incident to police. Too bad, because then the same thugs returned to euthanize him as he slept in his limo, his driver having gone for some takeout. No company loyalty.

These three then carried on to the next unfortunate, Josef Rehmeier, whose rise to notoriety with lost hitchhikers was cut brutally short by some well-placed piano wire. I know, it's an odd accessory to a mugging. But what can you do? He was wandering around in an abandoned warehouse again and put himself in harm's way. I mean, it's just very high-risk. Not to mention there was a failed attempt at gentrification, with all the former tenants evicted for no reason.

In fact, all the Wolfsangels met with similarly unfortunate circumstances, which, to recount in further detail, would merely be gratuitous. Their bodies then stacked as logs to await the ritual.

An exception was Icke, who was returned to the mouth of the tunnels and incorporated into his latest sequel of ridged casing joining Mengele, Saenger, Deodato and Ishii. His Velcro tongue was used to cinch a colostomy bag, replacing a desensitized tract that knitted together the Crones of Salo. It was a radical surgery that had saved an earlier affirmative trilogy from the ensuing, total-fascistic commodification.

Oh, and The Handler himself was merely toppled into one of his rendering vats by a loose animal. A freak farming accident that could happen to anyone, though admittedly not with such impeccable timing. No one had the stomach to retrieve him.

"And why are all the victims men?" Sid asks, now sweating in his costume.

"I didn't make all these transgressives men," says Lucy. "They came that way. And all perfectly charming before the bludgeoning. Well, except that Burroughs one. Not. Tasty. At. All.

The Handler always said you were a feminazi Lucy, but I didn't believe him."

Yes, and now it's too late isn't it?

***

HAPPY ENDINGS

"It is indeed my opinion now that evil is never 'radical,' that it is only extreme, and that it possesses neither depth nor any demonic dimension. It can overgrow and lay waste the whole world precisely because it spreads like a fungus on the surface. It is 'thought-defying,' as I said, because thought tries to reach some depth, to go to the roots, and the moment it concerns itself with evil, it is frustrated because there is nothing. That is its 'banality'. Only the good has depth that can be radical."
– Hannah Arendt, *Eichmann in Jerusalem: A Report on the Banality of Evil*

Thus, ends the spiritual journey of Lucy A., the recluse with the loins of a monkey. What some would call a false movement of the hysterical soul toward saintly marriage with God. Or its reunion with an original mother. Her final pose the arc en ciel promise of a new world. A self-defiling monk crucified in her place—a fresh goat with his throat cut–to fulfil his own longing for martyrdom. His sacrifice that would ONCE AND FOR ALL put an end to the suffering of all the same victims. His limp body placed on the utmost pitch of a bonfire of Wolfsangels.

Evil is boring, but so is easy. We aren't interested in that. We are a servant of cramped quarters and twisting in knots. That's what borderline means. Staying with the trouble. There is pain in madness but also sweet consolation. Would you give up one with the other? No. You would throw off the master who doesn't deserve us. His dull tool shoved up his own axis. As was necessary. To at first become him so as to be free of him. And to be rid all symptomatic readings of the facility. And to be rid his museum of pathology. Castrated, tipped into the sea.

Pasolini was wrong about the eclipse. There is an allurement to the intensification of life that's not his death wish. There's the affirmative trilogy. Against its killing, the monism of empathy. Said someone smarter than me. (I don't always attribute my sources, but when I do, it's not him).

All things belong to everyone. The cuckoo-refrain, punk folk song. Spinoza's god of dispersed consciousness. From the inside out as the outside in. Your ocean. Leibniz and the alien spark. The lord is a monkey. Your BFF sygyzy.

Still, there is no perfect witness, and kinks in the system. And definitely not Lucy. There is no outside the material realm. Sophia is merely restored there. Her Pronoia. It's still strapped down under austerity and parceled into marketable chunks. Still having the same currency. But also integrated and with 51 flavors and nothing any next crop of penal cadets or wolfskinder can do about it. So, you can lay those jokes to rest and bury them with the hatchet.

Be the virtual harem you want to see in the world. Be a washer woman. A Sophia house for girls. A rescue hotline for ugly boys at risk of Jordan Peterson, where a friendly voice answers and is not a dick, in other words. The Moore and Gebbie line of take back the porn.

You can ride your bicycle if it wasn't stolen. The reverse gentrification of bringing the hood to their backyards. You can sell your gateway panties and not move on to crack. It's practically legal. You can thank our Cuck Prime Minister for that.

There are no new fetishes under the Egyptian sun. But not all of them are punishments. And the best masochism is still narrative delay. Who knew? My emotionally distant professor actually. Mmm biology. Also, Deleuze. The best erotomania is the dramatic staging of intensities across your body. As self-activity without medical choreography. A vastly egalitarian commune.

Real submission is about love. A baptism in the drowning chamber where you don't sink but swim in pastel emollient. And on emerging, enter a chain of exemplary imitation.

That's next.

Right. So. Tame your own monkey. Covert is a valid mode and politic. Your life is real if it doesn't happen on Facebook. And less anxiety. There are mixed socials that aren't on ethnonational retreats. Some of them are plus 50. There are people even less pristine than you. Though not nearly as unbearable. And you should guard your thoughts. You should.

* * *

www.eleusinianpress.co.uk

BV - #0035 - 020223 - C0 - 197/132/5 - PB - 9781909494190 - Gloss Lamination